FORTY DAY FIANCÉ

ERIN MCCARTHY

ONE

I HAD DONE something so absolutely and utterly bonkers that I kept wondering if I could claim temporary insanity. Or temporary stupidity might be more accurate.

Because I was a catfisher.

The complete misrepresentation online of myself as another person entirely.

I hadn't meant to get so carried away. It was an accidental catfish.

What had started out as me finding a date for my friend Savannah had somehow resulted in me chatting on the app with a man named Michael for hours. Days. Maybe even a few weeks. As Savannah, not me, Felicia Hobbs.

It started out harmless enough. It was called *screening*. I was making certain he wasn't a psychopath. For her. I had an obligation as a friend to not send her off to dinner with a serial killer.

Then it got to where I was telling him my own stories and feelings and maybe even falling for him, just a little. Okay, a lot.

Which was ridiculous because he thought he was talking to Savannah. She was a peaches-and-cream-complexion redhead with a sweet smile and an overwhelming optimism. I was a thin, pale, dark-haired British ex-pat with a dry sense of humor and a practical streak.

One of these things was not like the other.

Do you see my dilemma? It was charming in Cyrano De Bergerac.

In real life, it was just rude and a little creepy.

The only explanation I had for it was I had spent too much time home alone, working. We are not meant to hole up for days on end in a bedroom the size of a car boot surrounded by mounds of vintage clothing. I'd become eccentric, reclusive, obviously craving a connection with someone.

It was an accident, truly.

Though generally speaking I was known for getting myself into cock-ups, I had to admit. It was why I'd stopped dating altogether the year before.

Michael and Savannah had gone out to dinner and she'd told me he was nice enough but she wasn't interested and, of course, that's because everyone but her knew at the time she was already totally in love with Maddox, her roommate and nanny.

I was certain she'd left Michael wondering why the hell she'd been so hot (me being she) and then cold in person.

I'd also been stupidly relieved she hadn't liked Michael and stupidly annoyed when he had continued to message Savannah, clearly interested in a second date, despite her tacit reaction to him. Was it her looks he liked, or me, the woman he'd been chatting with?

But he had mentioned early in our communications he wanted to get rid of his wife's clothing, given she'd been passed away for ten years, so after their date I'd got in the wine and told him, as Savannah, to contact me, Felicia, who would potentially buy some pieces in his wife's wardrobe.

See? Making it worse.

But now I was standing in front of an apartment door in SoHo hitting the buzzer for Dr. Michael Kincaid and feeling every ounce the idiot.

"Hello?"

"Yes, this is Felicia Hobbs."

The buzzer rang. "I'll come down and meet you in the lobby," he said.

He had a sexy voice, unfortunately. It was low, gravelly, the tone commanding.

I had thought altogether too long about my outfit, but it was December and I was bundled up with a long winter puffer coat, a beanie on my head. I'd had a decent struggle with myself over footwear, wanting to thumb my nose at the weather, but it was snowing and I didn't think an open-toed pump was going to accomplish anything other than a broken ankle. It wasn't like Michael was going to see the pumps and what they did to my legs (amazing things, truly) and decide he was mad for me.

Hence the waterproof high-knee boots with adequate treads. I wasn't going to shag the man, so what difference did it make?

It was called managing expectations.

I stood in the lobby, waiting for Michael to appear. It was what you'd expect for SoHo. Only eight units in the building and presumably all large and airy loft-style.

The lift opened and a man came out.

Michael was not as expected.

I'd seen his picture, but it hadn't captured that confidence in his step, that height, that sexy shot of silver at his temples. He was wearing jeans and a navy blue T-shirt, and a tattoo was visible on his bicep. I hadn't expected a tattoo at all. He had on sandals, like he'd been barefoot in his apartment and slipped them on to take the lift down. He was far more rugged than anticipated, with a polished veneer.

He was, quite simply, a man I would love to get naked and rub bits with.

I gave a little wave. "Hi, I'm Felicia. It's nice to meet you, Dr. Kincaid."

Then I realized I wasn't supposed to know what he looked like.

He didn't seem to notice though. "Call me Michael." He put

his hand out and gave me a smile. "Thanks for coming by. I hope this isn't a waste of your time."

I didn't care if he didn't have a single article of clothing of any value. I was getting a glimpse into his flat and into him. Which made me utterly hopeless. But I had a crush. We're allowed to have crushes at twenty-eight years old, aren't we?

"My pleasure," I said, and I meant that quite literally. "Based on the photo you sent, I'm optimistic we can find some gems in your wife's wardrobe."

"I know the basics of fashion," he said. "I can pair a tie with a suit, but when I'm not at work or at some sort of fundraiser, I'm well... " He gestured to his clothes. "Casual."

"Look at me," I said. "I'm wearing a puffer. I don't exactly look like I know my way around a runway, but I can assure you, I have the knowledge necessary to sell anything you'd like in my online store." When I had first arrived in New York, I'd had a dream of continuing my European career as a runway model because of how much I'd enjoyed fashion. I'd achieved some success, but I'd also spent two miserable years going to hundreds of casting calls and having agents dismiss me with barely a glance.

I'd learned not to take it personally, but it's never pleasant to be told your lips are repulsive and that your skin is sallow.

Given I had no talent for actual design, I'd taken my love of fashion and turned it into a business. I bought and then resold, after garments were repaired and styled.

Michael gave me a smile. "I think you look practical since it's snowing."

Practical. Lovely. No wonder my vagina was the road less traveled. There was a roadblock in front of it marked "practical." Men don't get hot for practical.

I should have worn the heels, consequences be damned.

Making a non-committal sound I followed him into the lift. I didn't like at all that we'd already chatted quite extensively and he didn't know it. To him, I was a total stranger. Not even the person on the other end of a dating app.

He also hadn't taken one look at me and decided he wanted to change that, so that was disappointing. He seemed friendly enough, but not on the verge of ravishing me.

"I should have done this years ago," he said. "The clothes seemed too nice to just toss and I kept putting it off. I didn't mean for a decade to go by."

"I'm sorry about your wife," I said, because it seemed the polite response.

"Thanks. It's been a long time. We were only married for two years. I would say at this point the relationship is a very fond memory and that mostly I'm sorry she didn't get a full life."

I'd got the impression in his messages that he wasn't a man holding on to his grief with both hands, but there had to be a reason he'd not had a serious relationship in the ten years since her passing.

"So you're online dating, then?" I asked.

Out with it. Just like that. Idiot.

But I couldn't resist.

His profile had disappeared weeks ago (I know, I know, why was I monitoring it?) and I was starting to think that he had found the woman of his dreams. If he had, I needed to know so I could stop fantasizing about him. Nothing else seemed to be working.

When the lift stopped at the third floor, the doors opened. He gestured for me to go first. "No. I decided it wasn't my thing. No one I talked to seemed like they were really interested in a relation-ship. Just lots of posturing and hookups." There was a touchpad to his front door and he punched in the code. "That's not what I'm looking for, so I deleted the app."

I stepped into his apartment. "I'm sorry it didn't work out with you and Savannah."

What can I say? I enjoy self-punishing. My mum would always tell me not to ask a question if I wasn't prepared to accept the answer. I still hadn't learned my lesson.

"Can I take your coat?" he asked, holding his hand out.

"Sure, thanks." I peeled it off, juggling my large bag. I had brought my tablet to do some quick price researching and to take photos.

He wasn't going to answer me about Savannah. Served me right.

The unit was gorgeous. Floor-to-ceiling windows with tons of natural light. There was raw ductwork at the ceiling and a wall of exposed brick. The floors were sealed concrete and the kitchen was open shelving with a sleek island. His furniture was casual and modern. It looked expensive, but lacking just a little in the personal touch. Like a designer had done it and hadn't quite caught on to who Michael was.

"It's a lovely place," I said.

"Thanks. I've been here twelve years now." He hung my coat in a wardrobe. "As for Savannah, that's part of why I deleted the app. I thought we were talking for real, actually getting to know each other, had made a connection, and then we met and she seemed disinterested. I'm sure it wasn't her fault, I probably read more into it. I'm out of the game." He kicked his sandals off and came into the apartment. "Do you want a glass of wine? I was about to open a bottle."

Uh, yes, I wanted wine.

I wasn't sure how I felt about his answer.

I couldn't tell if he was still hung up on Savannah or not. It had only been a couple of weeks since their date, but on the other hand, she'd only talked to him for a couple of weeks prior to their dinner. Or rather, I had only talked to him for a few weeks. Did that mean he was hung up on me? Convoluted. All of it.

"I'd love a glass of wine." I stayed near the door. "Should I take my boots off? They're a bit wet."

"It's up to you. The floors are concrete, so it won't hurt them, but there is a rug in Becca's closet."

"I'll take them off." I used the wall for leverage and yanked off my boots. I went into the kitchen where he was pouring red wine into two glasses. "You never stood a chance with Savannah, by the way, so that's not on you. She was already halfway in love with an old friend and was refusing to admit it."

Michael handed me a glass. I took a sip, waiting for him to react to what I'd said.

"That's interesting because she was definitely *sexual* with me in messages. I didn't misread that. But never mind, I don't want to talk about your friend or give the impression I'm criticizing her. Like I said, I'm out of the game. I'm a workaholic with rusty dating skills."

Great, I'd made Savannah out to be a flirt when it was me. I was the flirt who'd been tossing out sexual innuendos and wishing I could have sex with him.

He raised his glass. "Salut, Felicia."

"It was me," I blurted, because I was in agony over the whole rotten thing.

He stared at me blankly. "What was you?"

"I was the one being sexual with you. It was all me, never Savannah. Every message you ever got was from me."

I wished I hadn't taken my boots off.

Because he was probably going to open his mouth and say, "Bye, Felicia," and if I had my boots on still, I could make a faster escape.

MY WINEGLASS WAS hallway to my mouth and I just held it there, staring at the gorgeous fair-skinned brunette with the British accent in front of me. I was trying to wrap my head around what she'd just said. She had fucking catfished me? Who the hell would do that?

"Why would you pretend to be Savannah?"

It was actually her I'd been talking to. That gave me an unexpected jolt of desire. She was beautiful, with striking cheekbones and intriguing blue eyes. She certainly didn't need to pretend to be her friend because she was worried about her own attractiveness.

Felicia made even the knit beanie on her head somehow look glamorous and mysterious.

I took a sip of my wine, leaned on my island, and waited for whatever explanation was about to come my way. If I found out this was a con to steal money, I was going to be very disappointed. And super fucking pissed.

"Savannah has terrible taste in men," she started. "Absolutely horrific."

I raised my eyebrows. "I'm horrific? That seems harsh."

"No! No, no, that's not what I meant." She waved her hand. "*I* picked you. See, that was the plan from the get-go. My friends and I would each pick a date for Savannah because she's just so bad at it. I created her profile and, at first, I tried to channel her and I tried to keep things straightforward and not get too conversational but..." She bit her lip and wrinkled her nose. "Then I met you. Or you know, saw your picture and messaged you. And you were funny and intelligent and I might have forgot that I was being her when I started talking to you and was just being me."

She tilted her wineglass and stared down into it before looking up at me. "I sound completely daft, don't I?"

I tried to process what she had said. "I don't know what it sounds like, honestly." Well. It really sounded like bullshit I was too old for, but I was willing to hear her out.

"At first my thought was you'd be a perfect fit. She has a baby, you're older, you want a family. I thought it had some real potential. I wasn't planning to do anything more than just set up a meeting between the two of you." She ran her finger around the rim of the wineglass. "But then I admit, I got a crush on you, and I didn't even realize it at first."

That wasn't awful to hear. She certainly had seemed genuinely interested when we were messaging back and forth. "Those were all your thoughts, your memories, not hers?"

She nodded. "Yes. My gran really did have knee replacement surgery. I have no idea about Savannah's grandmother."

I was both flattered and amused. And a little annoyed. "It

never occurred to you that it would become an issue at some point?"

"I wasn't thinking. Look, I'm not some tragic woman lying just to fool someone. I just... let it go too far."

I still didn't get it. But I was prepared to press her about it. "So do you actually sell designer clothes or was that Savannah? Or you, being Savannah, or maybe just made up altogether?"

Her cheeks flooded with color. "I do actually sell clothes." She dug into her giant handbag and pulled out a business card. "Here. But I fully understand if you would like me to leave right now."

"Do you want to leave?" I asked, because I didn't think that I wanted her to.

"I should, considering I've just confessed to having a crush on you and lying about my identity, but no, I don't want to leave."

"So you really do love Russian authors, British rock, and Australian beaches?"

She nodded. "Yes. And I do hate pickles, self-checkout, and tequila."

I tried to mentally scroll through all of our conversations and ascribe them to the woman standing in front of me. It wasn't hard to see that it made more sense than the woman I'd gone to dinner with. The real Savannah. Who had been sweet but not as sharp-witted.

"You, Michael, love true crime novels, British rock as well, and Belize. You hate chewing gum, buffering on the internet, and people who are cruel to animals. Like, it gets you raging." She set her wine down on the quartz countertop. "It was me, I swear, and everything I wrote was the truth."

I studied her. She looked sincere. I'd really enjoyed talking to her and she clearly remembered our exchanges even though it had been a month back. They'd meant something to her, like they had to me. She was beautiful. I'd be an idiot to be offended over the fact that a woman a dozen years younger than me had found me interesting enough to carry on a charade like that. I wasn't thrilled about the deception but I was willing to see if she was a chronic liar or had just gotten carried away as she said.

"Then I guess you owe me a dinner date with the woman I was actually talking to," I said. "Because she and I were having a great conversation."

She tilted her head and gave me a small, but very sexy smile. "Oh, really? I owe you that?"

I nodded. "I think you do." I came around the island so I could be closer to her. I glanced at her lips. "You told me you have a policy of always kissing on the first date, remember? Just to test chemistry. I'll be expecting that as well."

"I see. You drive a hard bargain, sir," she said. "But I'm prepared to make restitution."

"Excellent." She really was gorgeous. She was wearing a red sweater that contrasted with her dark hair and showed off a slim build. I could definitely imagine kissing her and more. "How does Thursday sound?"

Felicia raised her eyebrows. "You don't waste time."

"No, I don't. And I don't have time for games." I'd already wasted a decade of my life focusing on my career only.

"Ouch. Duly noted. No more deception, I swear."

I wanted a relationship again. I wanted to be married, to wake up next to a woman who wanted to share her life with me. Over the years of being single I'd had a few hookups and a couple of women who had wanted a friends-with-benefits scenario and that had been perfect for me at the time. But now, I wanted more. I wanted to know a woman inside and out, to love every inch of her, to have the luxury of being able to touch her.

Ironic, really. I couldn't expect any woman to be on the same page with me. I wanted everything all at once as usual. It was how I'd been successful in my career. Go for it. Grab what I wanted by the balls.

I reached behind me for my wine. I took a sip and studied her.

Felicia slowly slid her tongue across her bottom lip under the scrutiny. Her eyes darkened. She leaned almost imperceptibly toward me.

She wanted me to kiss her. Not Thursday, but now.

So I did what I always did. I went for it.

I set my glass down and reached out and took her glass from her and set it next to mine on the island. I slid my hand into her dark, straight hair. "You're a very beautiful woman, Felicia. I've enjoyed talking to you, you little catfisher."

"I've enjoyed it as well."

Her voice was a low murmur, breathy, aroused.

I bent down and covered her lips with mine.

TWO

MICHAEL WAS KISSING ME. Holy shit, he was kissing me and it was brilliant.

I had thought telling him the truth would get me bounced from his flat, which would have gutted me, but instead he was kissing me. Very well, I might add.

He had soft lips and a commanding touch. His hand held my head while he brushed over my mouth over and over.

I kissed him back, but he was in charge, one hundred percent. My eyes drifted shut as he teased between my lips with his tongue and did all kinds of amazing things to my insides. I pressed my hands on his chest for balance and to feel him. It was a hard plane of muscle that only stoked the fire of my desire even further.

Curling my fingertips into the fabric of his T-shirt, I sighed, wanting to be closer to him. Wanting to feel every inch of him.

Michael broke off the kiss and stepped back from me. He gave me a slow, sexy smile.

"Let me show you that closet."

Just like that. Let me show you that closet. Like he hadn't just destroyed me with his mouth. Like he hadn't made me ache for more.

I stood there for a second, struck dumb, breathing hard.

He turned and sipped his wine.

That snapped me out of it. "Right. Of course. Let's get right on that."

The reason I was there. To assess his dead wife's wardrobe. Not to shatter beneath his tongue.

He didn't look shattered. He looked as casual as his outfit. Chill. Cool as a damn cucumber.

I reached into my bag and pulled out my tablet, determined to be professional for the next thirty minutes. "I'll just snap a few photos for reference. I can usually get you an estimate within three days of what I'll be able to take to list and target auction prices. If you choose to use my services, I will need to remove the clothing so that photos can be taken on a model with styling. I take forty percent of the sale price and do all the shipping."

"Sounds good to me. I'm planning to donate the money to breast cancer research."

Of course he was. Because that wasn't going to help my burning desire to shag him. The bastard was a nice guy on top of being attractive, intelligent, and forgiving.

I followed him down the hallway to the second door on the right. It was clearly intended to be the second bedroom but it was set up like a walk-in closet. It was all women's clothing. Hundreds of pieces. There was a rack of shoes that even at first glance showed designer taste. The shelves filled with handbags displayed a very obvious Chanel and a Hermès courchevel Birkin with gold hardware. Becca had a Birkin. I wondered if Michael had any idea how much just that one bag alone was worth.

"There are a lot of quality pieces here," I said, running my fingers down the sleeve of a Prada jacket. "How many are you willing to part with?"

"All of it."

My heart almost stopped. Turning in a circle I at first guess thought there was at least fifty thousand worth of designer pieces in the room. More likely even more. The Birkin alone was worth five grand gently used. This would be quite the padding for my bank account.

"This is thousands and thousands of dollars in fashion, do you realize that?"

He nodded, leaning on the doorway frame. "I bought most of it. Trust me, I'm well aware of how much it cost. That's why I figured I would have someone sell it and I'll donate the proceeds."

"Thank God you didn't throw all of this in the bin." The thought made my stomach hurt. "That would be a crime against fashion." The beauty of so much fabulous clothing was really the only thing that could have distracted me from my attraction to Michael and the fact that he'd kissed me.

There was still an awareness on my part of him filling the doorway, of our obvious easy chemistry, but the clothes were to die for. I shifted through the hanging dresses, jackets, and skirts. I pulled a few that I wanted to start with, trying to ignore the voice in the back of my head that was telling me going on a date with Michael was falling back into an old pattern I'd consciously tried to break.

The older man with money.

Been there, done that, and I had always wound up feeling less than. The power balance had always been off, and particularly back when I'd been modeling, it was clear my role was to be eye candy.

I'd known Michael was a doctor but I wouldn't have thought he was capable of buying a wardrobe like this one. Besides, I'd thought I was talking to him for Savannah, not me. It was obvious now given this flat and room full of fashion, orthopedic surgeons pocketed more money than I'd expected. Or maybe he came from money. Either way, warning bells were going off, but I resolutely ignored them. I'd already agreed to go to dinner with him. I couldn't be a complete idiot and cancel on him now.

"How long have you lived in New York?" Michael asked as I laid several dresses on the ottoman in the center of the room and took pictures so I could do some research.

"Off and on for eight years. I've spent stints in Vancouver,

London, Berlin, and Milan." Every year or so I had to leave temporarily to meet the pesky terms of my visa.

"Wow, quite the international woman. Here I thought you were from Pennsylvania."

I turned and make a face. I had to be prepared for him to tease me about being Savannah, but that didn't mean I had to like it. "I've never been to Pennsylvania but I'm sure it's delightful."

"What were you doing in Milan? I love Italy. I spent a month there two years ago."

"In my younger years, I did some modeling. I was a showroom model for Versace for fashion week." Becca was clearly not a Versace woman. I hadn't spotted any pieces from the iconic house. She was more of a conservative dresser. I, on the other hand, loved the glamorous sexuality of Versace. I just didn't have anywhere to wear it anymore.

"I'm not surprised you were a model, but you're saying 'younger years' to the wrong person." He gave me a grin. "That sounds ridiculous to me. What is a showroom model? I'm visualizing you lying on the hood of a car and, trust me, it's a good visual."

That made me stand up straight and give him an appalled glare. "What? Bite your tongue! It's where you stand in an outfit, perfectly still, for hours, while international buyers come in with the label and go through all the pieces. They want to see how the garments lie on a real body, not a mannequin. There is usually a half dozen models or so in a showroom and the buyers have appointments to view."

"That's not at all what I was picturing."

I laughed. "Clearly not. No, I was not lying on cars in a Union Jack bikini, sorry to disappoint."

"That is actually very disappointing. Did you enjoy showroom modeling?"

"God no, are you bonkers? It's boring as hell to stand there immobile, not speaking while they touch and prod the clothes you're wearing while saying things like 'I love the affordability of this' when it's a ten-thousand-euro jacket."

"That doesn't sound enjoyable at all."

"No." I snapped a pic of the Chanel Classic quilted single-flap in a caviar color. I put my hand on a drawer. "May I look inside?"

"Of course." He just watched me.

Inside there were velvet boxes with necklaces, bracelets, and earrings laid out.

I would be jealous of his wife except the poor woman had barely had time to enjoy her beautiful things. It made me feel instantly sad for her. What a hard knock, getting breast cancer at thirty.

Quickly, I took a few pictures then closed the drawer again. "I'm done," I said, wanting out of there. I could feel his eyes on the back of my head and it made me uncomfortable.

Besides, what if Becca's ghost had just seen me snog her husband and now I was picking through her clothes to sell them? I did not want to be haunted by a jealous ex. That was all I needed in my life.

"I'll have a quote in a few days and you can let me know if you want to proceed."

"Oh, I want to proceed," he said.

His voice was whisky smooth and dripping with innuendo. Presumably sexual. Or maybe that was wishful thinking on my part.

But I had to get out of there before I asked him to bend me over the ottoman. It had been far too long since I'd had sex and I really, really wanted to call him daddy.

Bye, Felicia.

As much as I hated the expression it had its appropriate moments and this was one of them.

Gripping my tablet against my chest, I eased past him out of the closet. For a second I didn't think he was going to move, that he was going to kiss me again, but then he shifted to allow me to exit.

I couldn't get out of there fast enough. I set my tablet down so I could stuff my feet into my boots and threw my coat over my arm. I'd put it on in the lobby.

"I'll call you about Thursday," he said. "Do you have a cuisine preference?"

"I'm fond of sushi. Speak to you soon." I opened the door to his flat and bolted for the lift.

"I'm looking forward to it," he called after me. "I'm looking forward to a lot of things."

His words might as well have been his tongue sliding over my clit. My puffer slid out of my hands to the floor. Damn it. I wasn't being smooth at all. I bent over and scooped it up.

As I took the lift down I typed into my group text thread with my girlfriends NEED TO CHAT, asap.

Current status required a cocktail and a girls' night.

"HOW'S the search for a surrogate going?" Sean asked me, eyeing me over his glass.

I knew exactly what my brother thought about me paying a woman to carry my baby. He thought it was insane. And part of me thought it was insane as well. But I wanted to be a father and I didn't want to spend the next five years trying to find and/or force a relationship to work just so I could have a child.

"I'm taking my time, doing a lot of research." I sipped my bourbon as we relaxed in my living room, take-out food spread on the coffee table in front of us. "I know you think this is crazy, but trust me, I know what I'm doing and I'm weighing all my options."

Sean was almost seven years younger than me and far more happy-go-lucky. He shook his head and gave me a grin. "Oh, I know you'll do that. You're the planner man. But I also know that you want what you want when you want it and sometimes that's not a good thing. This is a kid, not an impulsive trip to Bali."

"I'm well aware of the responsibility of being a parent. I told you if I do this, I'm taking a year off of work."

"Dr. Dad. I can't really picture it. I mean, I can picture you as a father, just not as a stay-at-home dad." He drained his bourbon. "What is this stuff? It's very smooth."

"It's like two hundred bucks a bottle. That's what it is. You're supposed to sip it, not shoot it." I demonstrated. "See? Sip. And why can't you see me staying home with a kid? I'm highly offended."

He snorted. "Have you thought about how you're supposed to date when you're raising a baby?"

I shrugged. "Speaking of dating, remember that woman I went to dinner with a month ago, Savannah? Turns out I was catfished."

"I remember her. The redhead. Why and how were you catfished if you met her and it was really her?"

"Her friend was the one who was actually messaging me." I pulled my phone out of my pocket. I had looked up Felicia after she had left and found her social media, including some of her old modeling shots. I pulled up a more recent photo, where she was modeling some of the clothes she had listed for sale. Her dark hair was in loose curls and she had on bright red lipstick and fake glasses. "This is her." I handed the phone to Sean. "We're going out Thursday."

"I hate you," Sean said. "Seriously, what the fuck, man? You got catfished by a woman who is actually attractive? That's unprecedented."

I knew he was right. I grinned and leaned forward and snagged a piece of shrimp. "She's gorgeous, isn't she? Her name's Felicia and she has a very cute British accent."

"She's more my age than yours. You're swimming in my pool, fucker. Go wade in your own."

"No way. Age is just a number."

"You're a douchebag."

"And you're a dick who is at least five years older than her anyway," I said good-naturedly. Sean and I got along great, always had. We had a sister, Maeve, who was in between us in age, but she lived in California now. Sean was a chef in Brooklyn and worked as many hours as I did, if not more, so we didn't get to hang out a lot but when we did we fell back on the old habit of giving each other shit. "How's your love life?"

He made a face. "Let's put it this way. If I ever get the urge to have children, I'll probably be calling your surrogate."

"We are not using the same surrogate. Our kids would be cousins and half-siblings. That's bizarre as hell. Why don't you jump on a dating app?"

"I'm on all of them. Easily six apps. It's like Wheel of Fucking. You spin, pick someone, and have sex. Then you ghost each other and move on to the next one."

"You could try conversation."

He made a sound. "What, like you? All that got you was a brunette pretending to be a redhead. Twenty bucks says she's flat-out crazy."

"It's entirely possible." I hoped not. But it was possible. A chirping sound occurred again for about the fifth time from somewhere in the apartment. "Do you hear that?" I said, distracted. "I keep hearing something beep, like a notification. Is that your phone?"

"No, mine are on silent." But he pulled his phone out and looked. "Definitely not me. Is it your phone?"

He'd set my phone on the coffee table after looking at Felicia's photo. "No. It's coming from over there somewhere." I gestured toward the door.

I stood up. It was driving me crazy. It was irregular. It would do it multiple times rapidly, then nothing for ten minutes. "It's not the smoke detector."

Then I spotted it. "Oh, Felicia left her tablet here. She must have forgotten it when she put her boots on." I picked it up, intending to turn it off or stick it in a drawer until I could return it so I didn't have to listen to the notifications pinging.

Only I realized that her texts were popping up in the right-hand corner and one included my name. Unless Felicia knew more than one Michael.

It would be wrong to shag Michael after one dinner, right? Tell me not to shag him.

Hell, yeah. The words went straight to my cock and I pictured Felicia naked in my bed, her dark hair spread across my white linen sheets.

"Look at this," I said to my brother. "She wants to have sex with me."

"You shouldn't be reading that." But Sean took the tablet anyway and said, "Damn. She's definitely DTF. Down to fuck. Plan accordingly."

I reached down and picked up my glass. I couldn't sit back down. I had a hard-on now. "She's crazy, isn't she? That has to be the catch." It seemed too good to be true.

"For wanting to have sex with you? Definitely."

"Shut up, dick. You know what I mean."

"Oh, for sure," he said, cheerfully. "Beautiful, single, lies easily. You could definitely wind up with a stalker."

THAT MADE me roll my eyes. "That seems like an overreaction."

"Crazy women are great in bed. Just enjoy the ride before she starts slowly and methodically ruining your life."

"I'm not worried about that." I wasn't actually worried about anything. I was excited. Intrigued.

"Her friends are mostly telling her not to have sex except the one is saying she can't really give advice on restraint since she had sex with her fiancé after he gave her a ride home." Sean looked up at me. "My kind of girl."

I gave a soft laugh. "Someday you're going to fall head over ass for a woman and I'm going to love watching you squirm and resist." I reached out for the tablet. "And you're right—we shouldn't be reading those."

"Even though she says if you came over right now, she'd ride you like a mechanical bull?"

Fuck. I got even harder. "She did not say that." Knowing Sean, he was just yanking my chain.

He shrugged. "Look for yourself. Trust me, I would not make that up." He handed me the tablet back.

I studied the screen. There it was. Almost word for word what Sean had said.

"Get out," I told him.

"What?" he asked, confused.

"You need to get the fuck out. I'm going to take this tablet back to her." Only a fucking idiot wouldn't take advantage of the opportunity.

"Right now?" Sean shook his head. "You can't do that. She'll know you read those texts and then you'll just look like an asshole. A horny asshole."

"No, she won't. We didn't open any of them. They just pop up, then disappear. When she logs in with her password they'll show on her tablet as unread. Besides, I'm sure she wants it back as soon as possible. She took pictures of Becca's clothes to list for sale."

"You still have Becca's clothes? That's not weird or anything."

"I didn't know what to do with them. I don't know. They're in her closet and I just kept the door shut." I didn't think it was that weird. Well. Maybe ten years made it kind of weird.

I grabbed my phone and called Felicia.

"Hello?"

She sounded breathless, like she was walking.

"I wanted to let you know you forgot your tablet here. Give me your address and I'll bring it to you."

"I did?" I could hear her rustling around. "Well, shit. I live in Washington Heights but I'm not even home yet, so don't worry about it tonight."

"Where are you?"

"Just passed Forty-second."

"You're only halfway home, then. Do you want to wait for me somewhere and I'll bring it to you?" I was worried she wasn't going to have what she needed for other clients. I wasn't worried about me. I'd been waiting ten years, I could wait another week.

"No, no, it's fine. Thanks. Oh, can I ring you back? My roommate is calling." Felicia sounded frazzled.

"Sure. Talk to you soon."

I ended the call. "You can stay. She's not even home, so she doesn't want me to bring it."

"Good, because I wasn't leaving." Sean put his feet on my coffee table.

"You are not the company I want tonight," I said wryly. "Now take this tablet away from me before I read any more of her texts."

Too late. One popped up on the screen.

I should have gone back to his flat and begged him to go down on me.

I groaned and tossed the tablet toward Sean. "Fuck."

"Damn," he said.

I couldn't take it. I had to let her know I could see the texts.

So I sent her a text of my own.

You should have.

Should have what?

Come back to my apartment. No begging necessary. I would have gone down on you.

The bubble came up, then disappeared. Then she sent a head exploding emoji.

I smiled. My phone rang.

It was Felicia.

THREE

READING Michael's text had made my heart jump into my throat and both my hands come off the pole I was clinging to on the subway. I needed to go back and reread my texts from the group message with my girlfriends. Oh my God. It was exactly what I had said.

And meant.

How the bloody hell could Michael know that?

I was mortified. I was embarrassed. I was very, very turned on.

So I rang him.

"Hi, Felicia."

"What the hell are you talking about?" I demanded, feeling both angry and flustered. "Why would you send me that text? It's highly unprofessional." As were every single one of my thoughts surrounding him.

"I can read your texts in the group text with your friends on your tablet."

My heart fell back down into my gut. Of course he could. The damn tablet was synced with my phone. That had never even occurred to me when I was texting with my friends. He had seen everything. "A gentleman wouldn't have read what I wrote."

"I didn't mean to. It just popped up when I was moving the

tablet. Besides, whoever said I'm a gentleman?"

The train slowed and without a grip on the pole, I pitched forward and collided with a man's back. I hooked an arm around the pole and tried to decipher what Michael was actually saying. "You seem like a gentleman. Or you did, until this. Savannah said you were very polite with her."

"I was trying to put my best foot forward. But I can be a really dirty bastard if I want to be."

He was killing me. I closed my eyes. Which only goes to show you how mad I was for the man and his cock because no one in their right mind ever closes their eyes on the train. I told myself not to say it. Just don't. If I said it and this went in the toilet, I could potentially lose the commission if he no longer wanted me selling Becca's clothes.

But we all know that I said it.

"I love a good dirty bastard," I said. "Even a dirty bastard that reads a woman's private texts."

"You pretended to be another woman," he pointed out. "For weeks."

I could not argue with that. "I did."

"So I guess we're both a little naughty, aren't we?" he said, his voice sounding low and gruff next to my ear. "Get off at the next stop and come back to my place. Did you eat dinner yet?"

I shook my head, then realized he couldn't see me. "No."

"I'll order something and open another bottle of wine. Then I'll go down on you."

I mean... was there really any reason to say no?

"It sounds like an offer I just can't refuse."

"I agree. See you soon?"

I was already shoving my way toward the door so I could maneuver off the train the second it stopped. "Yes."

As I ran down the platform to get back on in the opposite direction, I sent a text to my friends.

STOP TEXTING. I forgot my tablet at Michael's and HE CAN SEE ALL OUR TEXTS WHEN THEY POP UP.

Oh shit, was Leah's immediate response.

Dakota just sent me approximately seventeen laugh cry face emojis.

Savannah sent a gif that was a woman snapping her fingers and underneath was written "Oh, snap."

That had me both rolling my eyes and laughing as I jumped on the train going back downtown.

Isla texted last.

Only you.

That's all she wrote.

But she was right. I was the only one this would happen to. I was the Bridget Jones of our friend group. And not because I was British.

My giant handbag was pressed against my thigh. I'd made a stop at a favorite boutique in SoHo that had candles in brilliant scents and now my bag weighed about three hundred pounds. But I would lug the bastard around all night if it meant I got to have sex with Michael.

He better not be overpromising. I was fully prepared to demand the pleasure he had offered.

I imagined him between my thighs and my face got hot. My nipples got hard. My lady garden got wet. It had been ages since I'd had sex and ages since I had wanted a man like this.

Being a workaholic was something Michael and I had in common.

Clearly another thing we had in common was a burning desire for each other.

He'd adjusted to me being Savannah easily. Or Savannah being me, however you wanted to look at it. I should probably have been concerned about that but I was choosing to ignore it.

I could dissect all of that later, after I'd had at least two orgasms.

When I got to his building I texted him and he buzzed open the door.

Come on up.

In the lift, I yanked my beanie off and dug in my purse for a brush and gave it a good yanking through my long hair. I popped a mint in my mouth and chewed it quickly, then put on a nude lipstick. Fortunately with it being winter my skin was drier than usual and didn't need a blot, but I wished I had known I would be having sex when I'd woken up that morning. I would have chosen my underwear with more care.

As I got off the lift, Michael's door opened and a man came out.

I gave him a nervous smile, realizing if he had been in the flat with Michael, he knew precisely why I was showing up.

The grin he returned confirmed that. "Hi, Felicia, I'm Sean, Michael's brother."

"Oh, hi, nice to meet you. I see the resemblance." He had the same strong jaw and rich brown eyes.

"I'm the younger and better-looking brother," he said, winking.

Michael appeared in the doorway. "Sean, shut up and go home."

He gave me a look that made my inner thighs bloom with heat.

"I'm going. Have fun, kids. Nice to meet you, Felicia. Make sure my brother holds up his end of the bargain."

My cheeks got warm. Damn it. I hated to blush but Sean obviously knew everything and that was just a touch awkward. Nothing for it but to just own it. "I'll be very firm with him," I said. "Rest assured."

Sean laughed. "Good." He clapped his brother on the shoulder. "You're in trouble. Talk to you later, man."

He moved down the hallway and Michael gestured to his flat. "Come in, Felicia. It's good to see you again."

"See?" I said. "There it is. Polite."

"And that's a problem?" he asked, looking amused.

"No, it's just a smoke screen I wasn't prepared for. I like the combination though. A lot." I wasn't even bothering to be coy. Why should I? He'd read all my texts. There was no hiding what I wanted when I'd already literally spelled it out.

"I like that such a sweet and pretty face hides a devious mind." He shut the door behind him.

"Devious? That seems a stretch."

Michael stepped into my personal space and looked down at me. "Devious. Naughty. Sexy. Beautiful."

I had to tip my head to look up at him. "You make me sound very intriguing."

He nodded. "You are."

Then he cupped both of my cheeks with his hands and gave me a sensual kiss. Neither light nor hard, but that delicious in-between where your mouths meet like partners in a dance. I sighed in pleasure.

He broke off the kiss and said, "Let me take your bag and coat."

I'd teased him a little about being polite, but it was actually part of the reason I'd always been attracted to older men. They had manners. Of course, a lot of men my age did as well, but an equal number did not. "Thank you." I handed him my handbag and peeled off my coat.

"I wasn't expecting your bag to be so heavy." He hefted it up and down before setting it on his console table.

"I popped into a shop on Houston and bought six candles. They have the best scents."

"That explains it. I ordered you sushi. It should be here in a few minutes." He took my coat and hung it in the closet.

"Wow, that was nice of you." I was hungry, but I was also feeling a massive sense of anticipation. I wasn't sure I could sit through two hours of chat and dine without it being weird.

"Do you want a glass of wine?"

I nodded and reached down to take off my boots. This was like take two. We'd already done this once today.

Only this time the sexual tension crackled between us.

I followed him into the kitchen and watched him pour two glasses of wine. Again. "It's like we've done this before just three hours ago."

He laughed. "If something is worth doing, it's worth doing again." He handed me a glass. "Cheers."

We lightly tapped the glasses together.

"So tell me what I don't know about you," I said. "We talked quite a bit online, but there are plenty of gaps left to fill in."

"I grew up in Manhattan, did I tell you that?"

I shook my head. "No. So a true New Yorker, then."

"Go Yankees." He moved toward the sofa. "Let's sit down. How about you? Where did you grow up since it wasn't Pennsylvania?"

"I grew up in London, a posh kid with posh parents." I put my glass down on the coffee table and sat down. "Then when I was sixteen my father lost everything to gambling. Well, I guess he'd been losing for years, but that was the year it became impossible to hide it anymore. The bank took the townhouse, the country house, the fifteen-car collection, and my tuition check to private school bounced. My mother filed for divorce. Not that I blame her. That's a hell of a secret to keep for years."

"Wow, that sounds like it was very disruptive for you at that age."

It hadn't been a great time in my life, that was for damn sure. "It was. But it probably made me work harder than I would have otherwise. Those years and then modeling gave me a perspective and maturity I wouldn't have had. I was a bit of a brat as a girl."

"How is your relationship with your parents now?"

"Mum and I are fine, though we don't see each other in person that often. My father remarried a woman with money, and while I don't actively dislike him, we're not close." I picked up the wine. Talking about my father was never particularly comfortable. "My mother is the one who taught me about fashion. She was quite the shopper and socialite."

"My family has a lot of money as well," Michael said. "I was a rich kid too. Private schools, polo lessons, a vacation home out in the Hamptons. We were mostly left to raise ourselves, and I have to say, we didn't do that bad of a job. Sean is a head chef at a great restaurant in Brooklyn and my sister, Maeve, is in television production out in LA."

"To city kids raising themselves," I said, lifting my glass again. It was actually nice to be talking to someone who had a similar background.

Most of my friends were from suburban upbringings and they had shared experiences that were foreign to me, like the cul-de-sac.

"I wouldn't trade it for anything. I had a ton of freedom. We thought we were pretty cool back in the day."

"Are your parents still here?" I asked.

He nodded. "They still live in the same apartment I grew up in on Fifth Avenue. Classic Upper East Side."

I wondered if I would have thought he was hot when he was back in school. Then again, I'd been a toddler. "What made you want to be a doctor?"

"I like helping people and I like being in charge."

That made me laugh. "Well, that's honest."

He shrugged. "It's true. And I like the challenge of solving the puzzle. What is wrong and how do we fix it?"

His phone buzzed. "The sushi is here. I'll be right back."

As he went down to the lobby to get the delivery, I pulled my feet up onto the sofa and tucked them under my thighs. I looked around, searching again for any personal signs that this was Michael's home. Or rather, what it said about him. But it was just a showroom for the furniture. There were no personal photos sitting around, no treasures from vacations. Though I thought it said more that he was a minimalist than cold-hearted.

He'd have a heart attack if he saw the cluttered box I lived in. It was better now that Leah had moved out. I'd taken her room and turned it into my storage and mailing room. It was floor-to-ceiling shelves and racks filled with clothes, boxes, and tissue paper. Organized chaos. My bedroom had become the location of my photo shoots in bad weather. My preference was to shoot outside with a building behind the model but that wasn't always possible in the winter, so I had to keep my furniture to a minimum to make room.

My bed was a twin, which was ludicrous at my age, but it was a small room.

I'd been fretting about the additional rent, but the clothes Michael wanted sold were going to help out dramatically on that front.

I decided to wander down the hall to his bedroom. Maybe his personality was more apparent there. I passed Becca's closet and resisted the urge to pull the door closed. "I'm sorry," I said, just in case she was hanging about. "He's a very attractive man, as you know. You can't blame a girl for wanting an orgasm."

Fortunately, there was no answer. The lights didn't flicker either.

His bedroom was highly predictable. A big queen bed with a modern vibe.

The bed wasn't made though, which surprised me.

"I'm lazy in the morning," he said. "I never make the bed."

I jumped slightly. I hadn't heard him come up behind me. I turned. "We all have a flaw or two." His hands were empty. "Was there something wrong with the order?"

He shook his head. "It's ready in the kitchen." His eyes went to the bed. "Unless you'd rather stay in here first."

Nodding, I sank my teeth into my bottom lip. "I think I would."

"I'm really fucking happy to hear that."

He came over to me, and this time, the kiss was hard, demanding.

It made me instantly hot.

I raised my arms so I could wrap them around his neck, and he drew me closer, a tight grip on my hips. I felt his hard cock brush against my thigh. Yes. That was what I wanted.

So I wrapped my leg around his and opened my mouth for his tongue.

WHEN I HAD RETURNED to my apartment and found Felicia in my room staring at my bed, I had regretted ordering the sushi.

All I wanted to do was ease her down onto that bed and taste her everywhere.

Given that her leg was wrapped around mine and she was rocking her hips to get our bodies as close as possible, she wanted exactly what I wanted. Both of us naked as soon as possible.

As I kissed her, teasing my tongue between her lips, I shifted my hands around to grip her tight ass. She gave a low moan of approval, which turned me on even more, if that were at all possible.

She was different than anyone I'd ever met. She was both blunt and a mysterious puzzle. I definitely recognized the dry sense of humor she had displayed online but she was also more enigmatic than I'd been expecting.

Of course, maybe that was just because I'd thought I was talking to a redhead with a sweet smile, not this sultry brunette who was meeting me kiss for kiss, demanding and uninhibited.

"God, you feel good," I murmured when she broke away for a second, sliding her hands down my chest. She had a tight, small ass that fit in both of my hands easily, and firm thighs. I'd never thought of myself as having a type. I found a lot of women attractive for various reasons.

But there was something about Felicia that had me impatient, raw. I wanted to pin her down, yank her legs up, and drive into her with hard, pounding strokes.

Fighting the urge to do that, I drew my thumb across her bottom lip. "You're beautiful. But then, you already know that. So what I'd like to say instead is that I find you absolutely fascinating, Felicia."

She had dark eyes that revealed little other than desire. "I'll allow that," she said, the corner of her mouth turning up in a seductive smile.

The classic femme fatale in a spy movie. That's what she reminded me of.

Which meant I was probably about to have amazing sex, and then she'd betray me. I was willing to take the risk.

Reaching behind my head I yanked off my T-shirt. I wanted to feel her skin against mine. I bent down and kissed her again, shifting to taste and tease down the hollow of her elegant neck, and across her clavicle, shifting her sweater aside. She smelled faintly of a spicy perfume that reminded me of a European tea shop.

Her fingers explored, brushing across my chest, over to my biceps, squeezing lightly. Every second of the fucking one million hours I'd spent in the gym were worth that moment of feeling like she approved. She gave a low moan in the back of her throat.

"You're very hard," she murmured.

"That I am." In every sense of the word.

Easing my hands up to her waist, I slipped under her sweater. Her skin was cool, soft, her waist dipping in. I kept shifting my touch further north as I kissed her earlobe, pulling it between my teeth and giving a small nip. Her grip on my biceps tightened, nails digging into my flesh.

I only briefly brushed over her breasts. That wasn't my goal right now. I just wanted her sweater off. Gathering the fabric, I pulled back so I could shift it up and over her head. She shook her hair back off of her face as I gently tossed the sweater onto a leather chair I had in the corner of the room behind me. She was all creamy pale flesh and dark hair tumbling in waves over her skin.

Tracing a path with my hands over her shoulders, I eased the straps of her bra down. She didn't have a huge chest, but her tits were high and rounded in her red sheer and lace bra. Of course it would be red. She seemed like a woman who was always wearing sexy panties and bras and this proved it. Today had been a regular workday for her and here she was wearing underwear that made a man want to sin. They looked expensive as well. Felicia had good taste, but I already knew that.

Bending over, I kissed the soft flesh above the cup of her bra. She sighed in clear pleasure. I brushed my lips lower, over her nipple, teasing it into my mouth through the fabric. It was so sheer it was barely a barrier and I sucked on the taut bud, gripping her hips.

When I pulled back briefly to shift to the other nipple, her head was back, her eyes drifting closed.

"I feel that where it counts," she said, sounding breathy and aroused.

That made me laugh softly. "Good. You should."

I reached around her slim body and unhooked her bra. I tossed it behind me to join her sweater. Then I walked her back to the bed, scooped her up and deposited her in the middle of my mattress. I needed to see all of her and those tight jeans needed to be peeled off from a prone position instead of standing.

Before I joined her, I did unbutton my jeans but kept them zipped and pulled open my nightstand for a condom.

She was waiting patiently for me, one knee slightly lifted, as she rested on her elbows, topless. It was a pose, whether intentional or just instinctual from her modeling days. At either rate, it was sexy as hell and nearly destroyed my plans to take this slow, fully seduce her. It made me want to yank her pants down and drive my cock inside her.

I climbed onto the bed and put my knees on either side of hers, invading her space.

"You're overdressed for this party," I told her as I popped the snap on her jeans and took the zipper down.

"Damn, I just hate it when I incorrectly gauge the dress code," she said. "So embarrassing."

Peeling the jeans off was not quite the project I'd expected but wasn't a three-second job either. It took some effort. "I'm happy to help."

"Such the gentleman again."

"I have my moments."

"I can't wait to see your transformation into dirty bastard."

If she had any idea what I wanted to do to her, she would probably run.

Then again, maybe she wouldn't.

Easing her panties down I shifted lower so I could flip my tongue over her clit and ease inside her pussy.

Fuck me. She was already wet with want and I drew in the tangy scent of her arousal.

"Did you want to beg?" I asked her as I pulled back slightly to meet her gaze. "Wasn't that your fantasy? To beg me to eat your pussy?"

"I don't know that it was my fantasy so much as what I thought might be necessary."

"Yeah?" I blew warm air onto her clit. I stared at her sex, so pink and juicy and ready for me.

She shifted a little.

I massaged my thumbs over her inner thighs, but not touching where she wanted me to touch. The tease was getting a reaction from her.

"Michael."

"Yes?" I let my fingers drift over the folds of her pussy and I ran up and down over the silken smoothness.

"I thought you said no begging required."

She had a point. "You're right, I did. My apologies."

"Oh, no, I want to beg. I just wanted to point that out."

Damn. Felicia was fucking amazing.

I pressed a soft little kiss and sat back, not sure she was serious.

She was.

She ran her hands over her tits and down over her flat stomach until she found my head. Her fingers gripped my hair tightly, enough to cause pain.

Then she said, "Michael, I am begging you with everything inside me, please take me with your tongue. Please run it over my clit and slide it inside my pussy so that I can come. Please. I'll do *anything*."

I wanted to drag it out, to see how far she would go, but her words made me way too hard and way too desperate to taste her.

"How can I say no to that?" I asked.

Then I moved my mouth over her hot tight pussy and gave her what we both wanted.

FOUR

IT TOOK everything inside me not to instantly orgasm when Michael finally slid his tongue inside me. He made me so eager, so desperate. I wasn't one to shy away from a little dirty chatter but I wanted to push it with him. I wanted to be submissive and beg him even some more. I wanted to do things I'd never contemplated before, like call him daddy.

His touch made me feel like I was drowning, being dragged down under waves of pleasure, where you can't find the life raft.

Then I realized he was the life raft.

I needed to hold on to him.

I fell back fully onto the bed, gripping his head and let him shatter me.

It came as a swell, not a quick burst, but a crest that rocked me from the tips of my toes to my scalp.

The loud cry I gave ripped from my mouth before I could prevent it and didn't even sound like me. It was wild and free and sensual.

As I tried to find air to breathe, my thighs relaxing as I came back down off the high, Michael pulled away.

"That was the hottest fucking thing ever," he said, his voice fierce.

He gave me a look that I didn't entirely understand. I shivered a little under that commanding gaze, the room cold without his body heat over me.

I expected that he would move inside me, but he didn't. He ran his hands over my body, his gaze following the path. He started at my head, moved down over my cheeks, my shoulders, palming my breasts, pebbling my nipples. It was unexpected, and made me feel oddly cherished. Like we were lovers, in the truest sense.

He was different from other men and I found that very attractive.

His exploration continued, down over my hips, over my pussy, which he barely touched. Just that slight skimming though was enough for me to let out a soft moan. The anticipation was both delicious and devastating.

I needed him to complete me.

It was a thought that should have given me pause, but it didn't.

"I need you inside me," I said, lifting my hips in an open and obvious invitation.

"You're the girl who wants what she wants when she wants it, aren't you?" Michael took his jeans down and reached for a condom.

I'd thought I'd outgrown a lot of that trait, but right now I couldn't argue it because it was true. "And here I thought you'd want the same thing."

That should get a reaction and it did. He practically growled.

"Oh, I do. Trust me, I do." He took my left leg and hauled it onto his hip.

For a brief second I thought he was going to tease me further, when without warning, he entered my body on a hot, swift thrust.

"Yes, that's brilliant," I said, closing my eyes briefly, arms drifting up over my head. "You have an amazing cock."

He did. I hadn't got much of a look at it but what I was feeling was everything I could ask for and then some. Thick, pressing deep inside me.

Michael was moving with a slow, steady rhythm, and watching

me, which at first was unnerving. He didn't close his eyes or look at some spot behind me on the wall. He made full, intense eye contact.

It caused a myriad of emotions to crash over me. Arousal. Anxiety. The desire to give him a show. I licked my bottom lip slowly, then sank my teeth into it. His nostrils flared. I let my fingertips drift over and tease at my nipples.

He swore under his breath.

I raised my hips higher to feel every single inch of him.

The minutes drew out and I lost any sense of time, just concentrating on holding myself back, staving off my orgasm. My eyes closed, because if I looked at him, I would fall off the edge.

He knew it. "Open your eyes," he demanded gruffly. "Look at me when you come. You're going to come, Felicia, aren't you?"

I nodded, throat tight. My inner muscles were clenched down hard on him as I tried to regain control.

His hand went under my ass and he lifted me off the bed, taking himself as deep inside me as possible.

Then he didn't speak, just took me and watched while he did it.

My orgasm wasn't like the first. This was sharp, a teeth-grinding, heart-racing split second of ecstasy before it was over.

He immediately came, and it was obvious he'd been holding off on his own satisfaction to let me orgasm. Ever the gentleman. The thought made me smile.

Michael sighed and eased himself down onto the bed beside me. "Why does your smile look so devious right now?"

I turned onto my side. "You give me far too much credit. I was just thinking that it would appear you had waited for me to orgasm before you."

His eyebrows rose. "I did. Ladies first. Is that amusing to you?"

"It's just that you truly are a gentleman, and yes, for whatever reason I find that amusing. And very, very sexy."

"I find you very sexy."

He gave me a kiss, then went to remove the condom. He got

out of bed and walked to his en suite, clearly comfortable in his own skin, as well he should be. The man was in great shape. I admired him naked as I fluffed a pillow behind me. The question was, what now? He retreated into the bathroom briefly, then returned, a robe in his hand.

"For you," he said, draping it across the foot of the bed. "I refuse to let you get fully dressed again while we eat sushi."

My cheeks felt warm. Goose bumps rose on my skin. "And why is that?"

"Because I don't want you to leave after we eat. I want to convince you for a round two and if I have you in just a robe, I'm stacking the odds in my favor."

That amused me. "A man who plans ahead." I appreciated that he was straightforward. Now I knew how this evening was going to continue and end and that was reassuring. We'd eat, drink a little wine, tumble into bed a second time, then I would take an easy leave, with nothing awkward.

"I barely got to taste you," he said, running his gaze over the length of my body as he reached into his wardrobe and pulled out a loose pair of joggers. "I'm definitely planning ahead."

That sentence was meant to just be flirtatious, yet it made me sit straight up and reach for the robe, oddly unnerved and no idea why. Or actually, I knew why I just didn't want to admit it. I already had a crush on him before the sex. Now I knew our chemistry was amazing. It wouldn't take much for me to fall for him head over ass and that made me panic. "Where is this damn sushi you can't stop talking about? I'm famished."

Easing it around my shoulders, I found my panties clinging to the bottom of the duvet, a splash of red on the white. I slipped them on and stood up, belting the robe tightly. It was cashmere and felt like heaven against my skin. It was cozy, but as I moved, it was tactile and soft and added to the sensuality of the night. Even the idiotic robe was a turn-on.

It was ridiculous.

Michael pulled on the joggers without his boxer briefs and then a T-shirt went over his head. It read Stanford across the front.

"Is that where you went to uni?" I asked, crossing my arms over my chest.

"Yes. Then med school at Columbia."

I knew enough to know both were prestigious.

"You must have been a good student."

"I like a goal. It drives me."

Then he surprised me by reaching out and taking my hand. "Come on. I can't allow a guest to be famished. Let me feed you."

He meant it quite literally. As I offered to help as he pulled containers out of his refrigerator, he waved off my gesture.

"I've got it. But here, taste this." He popped open one of the lids and pulled chopsticks out of the drawer in his kitchen island.

Quality chopsticks that wouldn't leave that taste in your mouth like you'd just licked raw wood, which you had.

He picked up a roll, and before I could see or ask what it was, he had it at my lips. I opened out of instinct and he put the whole thing in my mouth.

I pulled back, trying to resist, but it was too late. I was forced to chew and swallow. It was tasty, but I shook my head at him. When I could finally speak again, I said, "God, what on earth, Michael? I can't put that much in my mouth at once."

The second the words left my mouth, I realized what I had said.

His eyebrows rose and he grinned. "No? Well, that's a fucking shame."

I rolled my eyes. "Men and their penis jokes. How utterly predictable."

He just laughed. "You would have been disappointed if I hadn't said it."

"I don't think I would have, actually, but if that makes you feel better, go on and believe that."

I wandered over to the sofa with an appetizer plate of sushi and a glass of wine so he wouldn't feel compelled to shove sashimi into my mouth. The art of oral sex was a different thing entirely from eating uncooked fish. Which didn't seem possible, but it was true.

The robe enveloped me and I tucked my feet under it on the sofa. "Are you Jewish?" I asked Michael as he sat down on the sofa next to me.

He shook his head. "No. Why? Are you?"

"No. But you haven't got one single ounce of Christmas in this apartment."

"Oh." He looked around his flat like it had never occurred to him. "I live alone. It seems like a lot of work to decorate for myself. Besides, everywhere I go it's being crammed down my throat."

"Ah, a Scrooge." I smiled at him to show him I wasn't serious. "Though I do see your point. My roommate and I have a wreath on our door and that's it, so I suppose I can't really judge. But that's mostly due to a lack of space. We live in a closet. I adore Christmas, personally. It's so cheerful."

"I could do a wreath on the door," he said, but reluctantly.

It was my turn to laugh. "You don't have to do anything. I was just curious. This is such a huge space, with all these windows, I would enjoy decorating it. It's no fun to try to put up a tree in a six-by-eight bedroom like mine."

"Isn't that the standard size of a jail cell?"

"Most likely. I wouldn't know though, fortunately." I picked up another roll and nibbled on it. The caviar on top started to roll off, so I used my tongue to stop its descent into my lap.

Michael made a sound and I realized I'd inadvertently been sexual.

So I licked again.

FELICIA WAS LOUNGED CAUSALLY on the couch in my robe, one leg sprawled out, the other tucked under the cashmere. The robe kept gaping in various places, giving me a glimpse of her red panties or her bare nipples. Her cheeks had a healthy glow from sex and her hair was tousled. The "just fucked" hairstyle.

I had woken up that morning never once thinking I'd end the day with a hot Brit in my bed, but I had learned to embrace opportunities in my life. So when she used her tongue on the caviar topping her sushi roll, I didn't even hesitate. I took a swallow of my wine to give her time to chew and then I shifted closer to her.

I enjoyed talking to Felicia. Casual conversation was easy, natural.

But right now, I did not want to discuss my lack of holiday décor.

Easing my robe apart to expose her breasts, I brushed my thumb over one of her nipples. "I'm not trying to rush you, but are you done eating?"

"How is that not rushing me?" She pushed my chest and gave me a look that went straight to my cock. "A woman is done when she tells you she's done."

Why did that sound so fucking hot? "Understood." But I didn't stop teasing at her nipple. Instead, I cupped the small swell of her breast and squeezed, just a little.

Felicia picked up another roll, took a very tiny bite and chewed. "I'm done."

I almost laughed. But I just took the roll out of her hand and set it down on the coffee table. "It's about fucking time."

She did laugh. "Impatient bastard."

"I've been called worse things." I dropped my mouth over her breast and drew her nipple into my mouth so I could tease and tug at the taut bud.

Her fingers drifted into my hair. I shifted, kissing her neck, her earlobe.

When I kissed her on the lips she sighed and ran her touch down my shoulders.

Then she pushed me away again.

"What?" I asked, searching her face. Maybe she was a one-and-done kind of woman.

"Take your shirt off, please."

That was an easy order to follow. "Sure." I peeled it off and dropped it onto my concrete floor.

She was resting against the back of the couch, the robe still belted, but pulled apart at her chest and gaping at her inner thighs. She had a mysterious, naughty little expression on her face that seriously turned me on. I reached for her.

She held her hand up. "Take your pants off too."

Was this where she somehow handcuffed me to the coffee table and robbed me blind? It felt a little bit like that. It also felt a little bit like there was no fucking way I was going to say no. Let her take my money if that was her intent. At least I'd had fun getting conned.

"Whatever you say." I ditched the sweats.

Felicia pushed on my chest again, only this time, she straddled me, so I realized what she wanted was me on my back. And her on top. I decided to let her because she looked so pleased with herself, ordering me around. Wait until it was my turn to be in charge.

"You're very handsome," she said, as she ran her hands over my chest. "In case I hadn't mentioned that."

"Thanks." Amused, I held her waist and watched her explore her way down my body.

She wrapped her hand around my cock. "And this... this is very impressive."

My cock jumped in appreciation and got even harder. "What do you want more, to suck me or to fuck me?"

"Why be forced to choose?" she asked. "I'll do one, and then the other."

Hell yeah. "I have no objections to that plan."

The view of her dark hair spilling over my chest and her ass in those tiny red panties rising behind her as she shifted over my cock was one I wasn't going to forget for a long time. It was a fantasy sprung to life. I wrapped her hair around my fingers and tugged a little, wanting to assert some dominance even when she was in the power position.

Her tongue flicked over the tip of my cock and lithe fingers brushed over my balls, testing, teasing. When she eased her mouth down the length of my shaft, I gave her an encouraging moan. "That's it, baby. Take it all."

She glanced up at me from under her dark lashes, her lips wrapped around my cock.

Then she winked at me.

Holy shit, she was the most fascinating woman I'd ever met. I couldn't predict anything she was going to do or say and that should be unnerving, but it wasn't. It was exciting.

She dropped her head again and as she sucked me in and out I gripped her hair harder. I could feel the pull of her touch all the way into my balls. Damn, she was trying to destroy me.

"Felicia," I said, voice rough. "That's enough."

For a second I didn't think she was going to stop. It was a good thing I wasn't twenty-one anymore. I had control over myself. But then she drew back and let go of my cock with one final slide of her tongue across the tip. Her expression was smug as she wiped her lips off.

"Yum," she said.

She was definitely going to kill me. "Hand me a condom," I said.

She was already shimmying out of her panties.

"I've got it." She grabbed a foil packet off the table and opened it. She then started to roll it down on my cock.

I put my hand over hers so that we could do it together. It wasn't in my nature to be still. I needed to be part of the action.

Which was why once she eased her wet pussy down onto me, I let her have a minute or two of rolling her hips and fucking me, but then I took her waist with my hands and forced her still. I wanted more, faster, harder. I set a pounding rhythm and she moaned, her fingers splayed across her breasts, teasing at her own nipples.

Her lips were naturally full and they were red and glistening from our kisses and her sucking my cock. Her cheeks were flushed with arousal, her hair bouncing over her shoulders from our movement. Everything about it was a beautiful portrait of a gorgeous woman enjoying sex.

It was hard as hell to hold off, but I waited until she shattered on me. Her head fell back, her eyes drifting closed, a soft cry escaping.

That was all I needed, to see her satisfied. It sent me over the edge.

She fell onto my chest. I wrapped my arm around her back to hold her warm skin close to mine. We both just stayed that way, not speaking, breathing hard.

"I'm glad I forgot my tablet," she finally murmured. "And sent a group text saying I wanted to shag you."

I laughed softly. "Me, too, baby. Me too."

I was content to stay that way for a while but Felicia shifted off of me with a sigh and reached for her wine. She took a small sip and gathered the robe tighter around her. "I suppose I should head home."

That kind of surprised me. Did I give that kind of a vibe that I'd want her to leave immediately? "You can stay here if you want. It's cold outside."

But she waved her hand. "I really should go. I have a lot of work to do and I didn't plan for an overnight stay. I don't have a bag."

I wasn't going to try to talk her into it. I could respect that she wanted to be in her own space. "I understand. Let me call you a car when you're ready."

She gave me a kiss. "Brilliant."

I was feeling content, so I stayed on the couch, naked, finishing my wine while she went into the bathroom and got dressed. "Take this sushi with you," I said, boxing it back up. "Lunch tomorrow."

Felicia gave me a look.

"What?" I asked, dragging my sweats on. I was going to order her a car and walk her downstairs.

"Nothing." She sat in the club chair and pulled her boots on.

By the time I had my shirt back on and my feet in sandals, she had her coat on, her bag over her arm. She seemed eager to leave. I put the take-out boxes back into the plastic bag they're arrived in and tied the top off.

We didn't say anything as we rode the elevator down but it didn't feel awkward. Not to me, anyway. I hoped she didn't feel awkward, though I doubted a woman who winked during a blow job was one to feel regret or uncomfortableness.

In the lobby, we saw her car pull up. The doorman opened the door.

"I'll talk to you soon," Felicia said. "Thanks, Michael."

"I'm walking you out," I said.

"You don't have a coat on and you're wearing sandals. It's fine."

"I'm walking you out." I gestured for her to go first and she did. My doorman was studiously trying to not listen.

She rolled her eyes but obeyed.

I opened the car door for her. "Thursday at seven?"

The look she gave me was one of surprise, like she hadn't expected me to still want to do dinner. But then she nodded.

"Good night." I closed the door and waited until the car pulled away before returning to my apartment.

The doorman's name was Sergio and he and I chatted often about basketball, so it didn't surprise me when he gave me a grin. "Lovely lady, Dr. Kincaid."

I couldn't help but grin back. "Very lovely lady."

One that I hoped to spend a lot more time with.

FIVE

WHEN I PUT the key in and entered my flat, Javier was straight in front of me at the kitchen sink. "Hey," I said. "Did you miss me?"

He glanced back at me. "I actually thought you were in your room, so I guess the answer is no." He raised his eyebrows. "And where have *you* been? Savannah's? You don't usually get home so late on a random Tuesday."

"I was having sex with my new client," I said, determined to be breezy about the whole thing.

"Wait, a new clothing client, or is this your way of announcing you've joined an escort service?"

I laughed. "Oh, shut up. A new clothing client. The guy I tried to set Savannah up a ways back. They didn't hit it off."

"Apparently you did." He fully turned, a plate in his hand that he was drying. "Was it fun?"

"Very." My cheeks felt hot just thinking about it. I peeled my puffer off and threw it over my arm. "We had sushi and wine and *lots* of fun."

"Congrats. Hey, you need to open your mail." He tilted his head. "You got another very official-looking envelope from Immigration today. That's the third one and you haven't even opened the first two."

Shit. That was a mood killer. "How do you know I haven't opened them?"

"Because they are still lying here on the only fucking twelve inches of countertop we have in this kitchen. You're terrible at processing mail. I finally went through the pile because it was out of control and threw away your junk mail, and basically all you're left with is the world's biggest catalog from the shipping company you use for your business and three "Open me, bitch" type envelopes from Immigration."

A tremor of fear went through me. I'd been intentionally avoiding those envelopes. They were never filled with great news. No "Congrats, you've won free citizenship!"

"You're so aggressive," I complained, dropping my bag and coat on the floor. "This could have waited until tomorrow. You're ruining my post-shag glow."

"You're ruining my ability to chop vegetables."

I rolled my eyes and grabbed the pile he was referring to. "You don't chop vegetables."

"I would if I had counter space."

"Bloody unlikely." I bit my lip and ripped the top of the envelope off. "And there are only two envelopes, not three."

For a second as I scanned it, I told myself I wasn't reading what I was. So I read it again. And a third time.

The blood drained from my face. I got dizzy and hot.

"What does it say?"

"I'm being deported," I said, my voice a strangled whisper. "In forty days. Unless I can provide a reason why I shouldn't be, such as an engagement or marriage to a citizen."

"Um... that sucks. Can't you contest it or protest it or something? I thought you had permission to be here."

"I do. I did." I winced and shoved the offending letter in my bag. "It would seem I'm at the end of my visa. What happened to my extension? I applied for it at least two months ago."

I shifted through the pile to the other two envelopes. One was from Immigration. One was *to* Immigration. "Oh shit. I think this is my extension application. It never got mailed."

"Felicia, what the fuck?" Javier looked outraged. "How could you let that happen?"

"I don't know!" I wrung my hands. "I mail two dozen packages a week. They all are picked up by the mailman. This should have been in that lot ages ago!"

"It's been sitting on the counter the whole damn time. How could you not at least go through the pile and realize your mistake?"

I had no idea. I had been so certain that envelope had gone out with the packages, but obviously not. "I've been busy and you know I'm a massive idiot when it comes to things like that. I blame my parents."

"You can't blame your parents for not renewing your own visa when you're damn near thirty years old."

I had actually been kidding. Of course I didn't blame my parents. "What can I say, I'm a cock-up! I *meant* to. I filled out the application! But I get my head into work and I live it and breathe it, and I get surrounded by clothes and boxes and sales money dropping into my account and that is what happens. Not, you know, opening my mail." I ripped open the one envelope that had apparently arrived earlier, though I wasn't sure when. "It was a minor clerical error. To be fair, I thought I still had at least another month, which technically I do, so I wasn't concerned that I hadn't heard back yet. Haven't you ever let your driver's license expire?"

"Yes, but that only resulted in me being charged an extra fee when I went to get it. It didn't get me bounced from the country." He tossed the towel over his shoulder and leaned against the sink, crossing his ankles. He looked genuinely concerned. "What are you going to do?"

The greater issue over the expiration date was I doubted they'd grant me an extension at this point. More likely, I'd have to go back to the UK and apply for a new visitor visa. Unless Javier could save my behind.

"Ask you to marry me," I said, already knowing what his answer would be. It was worth a shot though. "We've been living together for eighteen months. It would come across as very legitimate."

His jaw dropped. Javier shook his head. "I have a girlfriend. I am not marrying you to fix your 'minor clerical error.' Shannon would kill me. Or *worse*, break up with me."

"She'll understand." I knew it was a losing battle, but I was desperate.

"What woman would understand that?" He gaped at me. "I would have to publicly break up with her on all my social media because the Immigration office would want proof that you and I are an actual couple. And you think she's just going to be cool with that? Are you nuts?" He opened the fridge. "I need a beer. No, sorry, I can't do it. I would ruin my relationship with Shannon and in the long run the whole thing would fail."

"Oh my God, you're right. I'm sorry, I can't expect you to save my ass." I sagged against the wall. "What am I going to do?"

"Ask someone who hasn't been in a recent relationship so you can fake one. What about your hookup tonight?" He drained half of his beer bottle. "You need to sort this shit out. I fucking cannot afford this apartment on my own and I don't want two random-ass people moving in here with me."

I frowned at him. "Glad to see you're going to miss the rent money as opposed to say, *me*."

"Don't be tender. This is the real world, little girl. Of course I'll miss you. Now find a solution."

It was like a proverbial drink thrown in my face. Javi was right. I needed to find a solution. "You're right. Sorry, I'm just freaking out. I don't want you to ruin your relationship with Shannon."

"Let's come up with a list of candidates. Who was the client tonight? Is he single?"

"Are you daft? I fucked him! Of course he's single." I was scandalized. I was never one to play the cheat.

"Just checking. Does he look good on paper?"

"He's an orthopedic surgeon, a widower, forty-two years old. But why on earth would he agree to marry me? We barely know each other." I didn't hate the idea. It was insane, of course, and presumably temporary, but it was oddly appealing. I enjoyed Michael's company.

But it was marriage we were talking about, not sushi and sex.

Actually, not real marriage. Just a fake engagement to buy me time to sort this out. But why the hell would Michael ever agree to something like that? He wouldn't.

"Stranger things have happened. But you're right. There isn't exactly an incentive there besides the ability to have you as a snack whenever he wants."

I wrinkled my nose. "Well, isn't that a charming way to put it? No. He's off the list. I will not sell myself as a bed warmer to stay in New York. I'll just go home to London." Where I hadn't lived in nearly a decade, had no real friends to speak of, a viral video scandal, and a father I did not want to see.

"There is always that. What about any of your other guy friends here?"

I mentally scrolled through our crowd. "They're all gay or in a relationship. I honestly don't have a huge friend roster, you know that. I live like a hermit."

"You do. I mean, I didn't even know you weren't home tonight. I assumed you were in your room."

"You're doing an excellent job of both making me feel better and problem solving, thanks so much. Bravo, Javier." I rolled my eyes at him.

My phone chirped in my bag and I pulled it out, needing a distraction. It was a text from Michael asking if I'd made it home okay.

Yes, thanks, I appreciate it.

I'll see you Thursday, then.

Right.

Is everything okay?

Yes, just got some off-putting news from INS.

Oh, no, sorry to hear that. What's going on?

I debated if I should tell Michael or not, then figured he had the right to now. He might choose not to see me anymore if I was going to disappear in a month. He was looking for a relationship, after all.

Wait a minute.

He was looking for a relationship.

So, maybe he wouldn't think getting engaged was completely insane? I decided to tell him what was happening.

It seems I might get deported.

What? Do you have a lawyer? Or need help finding one?

I definitely needed a lawyer. Or you know, a husband.

Maybe. I'll let you know at dinner. Thanks, xxx

Let me know if you want to talk tomorrow. Good night, Felicia.

"Why are you a hermit?" Javier asked. "I thought you used to be the girl about town? That's the way everyone still describes you, you know."

That was a story I didn't really want to get into. It involved a man I'd dated and the wife I hadn't known existed along with some rather embarrassing video that had briefly gone viral. Precisely the reason why I didn't want to go back to London. I was a bit of a social pariah at the moment through no fault of my own. Well, my fault in the sense that I'd chosen a man to date who was an utter asshole.

"I don't have time to be a lay-about." That was as much as I wanted to get into it with Javier. He was a great roommate and friend, but he wasn't the most sympathetic creature on the planet.

"I wasn't talking about being lazy. I was talking about socializing."

"Hmm. Right." I bent over and scooped up my bag and coat. "I'm off to bed."

"You can't avoid everything, you know," he called after me. "It's a life philosophy that will get you deported."

He was right, of course.

But I was my father's daughter.

FELICIA HAD TRIED to cancel our dinner plans earlier Thursday afternoon, calling me and telling me she was too upset to be good company.

"Is it that bad? Are you really being deported?" I had asked her, staring at the images on my laptop she'd sent me. It was her, modeling the clothes I'd had sent over to her apartment on Wednesday.

The shots were for her auction site, and she'd apologized that she would have tried to use a different model given the circumstances, but that her two regulars she used were the wrong size for Becca's clothes. Several of the dresses I honestly didn't even remember. There was one I did, but it stood out for all the wrong reasons. Becca had actually been angry with me the night she'd worn it to a fundraiser for the hospital. We'd had a fight about her spending habits and she'd bought it to be defiant. It was red, which was not a color she ever wore, but it had been done to stand out in a sea of dresses in what would undoubtedly be ivories, blacks, and blues.

I still didn't associate red with Becca.

But I did with Felicia.

I swiped through the images quickly in my office, not really caring about the lighting and the overall appearance, which was what Felicia wanted me to approve. They all looked fine and I was sure she knew what she was doing and could get them sold. None of that mattered.

All I could think about was how much she intrigued me, how amazing the sex had been, and how soon she was going to be leaving New York.

"It's that bad. I'm really being deported. I have forty days unless something changes."

I swiveled in my chair. I only had about five minutes. I had a meeting with the orthopedic department head. "I don't like the sound of that. What would need to change?"

"Either I have the world's greatest lawyer who convinces the INS that somehow I'm special and worthy of bending the rules because my contribution to the States is just absolutely extraordinary. I think we can see how that is going to turn out. A monster failure."

That made me frown. Really? I finally found a woman I could see exploring a relationship with and she was being sent out of the country. "How do you feel about going back to England?"

"It's not my first choice. I burned a bridge or two across the pond. But mostly, my adult life is here in New York. I haven't lived in London for more than a few months since my twatty teen years."

Normally that would have made me laugh but I was too pissed off. "There's no other way you can stay? Maybe as a fugitive or under a false name?" I was tempted to hide her in my apartment.

She laughed. "I'm not much for subterfuge, though I do love a good spy wardrobe. But I'm a bit of an idiot if you hadn't noticed. I couldn't pull out the lie long term. No, the only way to stay is to get engaged to an American. I asked my roommate Javier and he gave me a shockingly resounding no. I was quite offended."

Get engaged? Interesting.

"How could anyone say no to you?" I said.

"Quite easily. But Javier has a girlfriend, so I can't blame him. I need someone single for it to be believable."

"Did you have someone in mind?" My thoughts started to churn.

"I can't think of a single soul," she said.

Yet she sounded almost... flirty.

My surgical assistant popped her head in. "Are you ready?" she asked.

"Yes, be there in a minute, Kim, thanks.

"Felicia, I have to run to a meeting, but don't cancel dinner. I want to see you. It will be a great distraction for you."

"A great distraction? How could I say no to that?"

"You can't. Remember that. You can never say no to me."

She laughed. "Idiot. I'll see you at seven."

We ended the call and I stared at my phone for a second, before shaking my thoughts off. I stood up to head to my meeting.

A crazy idea was running through my head.

A very fucking crazy, sexy, dangerous, highly appealing idea.

SIX

MICHAEL WAS one hundred percent right. I needed a distraction from my impending exit from the States. I wondered how that worked. Did an INS officer escort me to JFK and I was put on a plane? Not that I would wait for that to happen. I wasn't going to resist if it came to all that. I didn't fancy being handcuffed to an air marshal.

All day I'd been working on listing the auctions for Michael's clothes (well, Becca's but it felt weird to think about his wife), trying not to think about it but the truth was nothing could fully distract me.

Except maybe a cocktail and sex.

We were meeting on the Upper East Side on his suggestion, so we were somewhat midway between our apartments and that was a bit disappointing. I didn't see much shag potential there if we had to go all the way downtown after dinner. Maybe he was trying to make it seem like he wasn't expecting sex. He was polite, after all.

It was actually something quite charming about him.

That didn't mean I didn't want to have sex though and I was not taking him to my place. It would be like having sex in a fitting room.

I stepped out of my Lyft and smoothed my skirt. Weather be

damned. I'd worn a dress and over-the-knee boots with a wool trench. I wanted to make the man drool.

Instead of going with a small clutch appropriate for dinner, I'd gone massive tote so while it still went with my outerwear, I could slip some overnight things in. Just in case. Toothbrush, deodorant, facial cleanser. Clean panties.

Michael was waiting in the entrance to the restaurant. It was a perfect choice for a cold winter night. Sicilian cuisine with a cozy ambience. Upscale, but in a classic way, as opposed to trendy.

"Hi," he said, giving me a kiss on the cheek. "Let me get your coat."

When he took it off and I turned around, his eyebrows rose. "Wow. You look gorgeous."

His eyes darkened with desire at my fitted sheath dress in black and the leather boots. I felt victorious. That look was worth the potential for a broken ankle. Besides, I'd only been outside for a couple of steps in each direction. Minimal risk. "Thank you. I decided just because I'm internally having a meltdown doesn't mean I should let that be reflected externally."

"I appreciate the effort." Michael gave my coat to the hostess. He was wearing dress pants and a shirt and jacket without a tie.

"How was work?" I asked.

"Boring. No surgery today. Just endless meetings." He put his hand on the small of my back and guided me to follow the hostess.

The table was tucked in the middle of the restaurant against an exposed brick wall.

"How are you holding up?" he asked, after he held my chair out for me.

I sighed, making sure to keep my shoulders relaxed. I didn't want them up around my ears while we were having dinner. "There's nothing for it, right?" I smiled up at the waitress as she approached. "I'll take a glass of pinot noir, please." No use in pretending I didn't want it immediately if not sooner.

"Let's order a bottle." Michael asked for a wine list.

The waitress mentioned a few options and they discussed it

back and forth while I zoned out. It felt very natural to spend time with Michael and that annoyed the hell out of me. One, because it was looking virtually impossible for me to stay in New York. Two, that I'd done it again. Chosen an older man with money who slowed down my wine order by the need to make sure it was the best option. And I didn't even care. He could order whatever he wanted as long as it was red and liquid. But that wasn't the point. The point was first it was wine, then it was "I forbid you to cut your hair, and have you gained weight?"

I didn't know he would be like that, obviously, but I'd dated enough to suggest that was a strong possibility when there was an age and financial gap.

Not that it mattered. We were going to have a few weeks to hang out, at the most.

It also meant he would be a great candidate to be my fake fiancé because I had reasons to stay emotionally distant.

"What do you think?" Michael asked me. "What's your preference, Felicia?"

Given I hadn't been listening to the waitress's suggestions, I just shook my head a little. "Oh, whichever you think is best."

Bloody hell. I mentally berated myself.

Maybe it was a good thing I had to leave the States because I couldn't be trusted not to be an accidental sugar baby.

But the thought of leaving made my stomach clench into knots.

"We'll take the Italian cabernet sauvignon." Michael turned to me. "If the lady approves."

The lady wanted him to stop being everything I shouldn't, yet did in fact, want.

"Sounds wonderful," I said, giving the waitress a smile. "Thank you."

She nodded and disappeared.

I glanced at the front of the restaurant. "I love this neighborhood. I know everyone wants to be in Brooklyn now, but I'm past my going-to-the-bar years, and uptown reminds me of my childhood."

"If you could live anywhere in the city, money no object, where would it be?"

That made me laugh. "Money is no object? Well, that's just absurd, so I don't know. Maybe a brownstone on the Upper West Side or something super traditional on the Upper East Side. Am I married with children in this fantasy or am I me as I am right now?" That definitely made a difference.

"Let's say you're married with the potential for children."

"I'll take the brownstone." I'd grown up in a brownstone but I didn't want to think about that and get melancholy. I'd loved the winding stairs and narrow rooms. So many nooks and crannies in that house. "I grew up in one."

"I grew up in this neighborhood."

"Oh, that's right. We're not going to bump into your parents, are we? That could be awkward."

"I didn't actually think about it, but I guess it is technically possible, though doubtful. It wouldn't be awkward, though, I get along with my parents and I'm a grown man. I'm sure they realize I date." He gave me a wicked smile. "It's not like I'm going to tell them how fantastic you look naked and how much I enjoy going down on you."

That went straight to my inner thighs. But I gave him a wry look. "How utterly disappointing."

Our wine arrived, and after it was poured, I raised my glass. "To you going down on me."

Michael laughed. "I'll drink to that."

I took a sip of the cabernet.

"And here's to you staying in New York."

That soured the moment. "I really don't see how that's possible unless you have a fiancé for me somewhere. Maybe tucked in your pocket?"

"I do," he said. "Me."

I choked on my wine. I coughed into my fist and set my glass down, staring at Michael. "I'm sorry, what on earth are you talking about? What do you even mean?"

He shrugged, like he hadn't just suggested we get married. Or pretend to intend to marry. While I had seriously contemplated a fake engagement to Michael I never in a million years would have thought *he'd* be the one to suggest it.

"You need a fiancé. I happen to be available. I like spending time with you and we clearly have chemistry."

I agreed with that, but what I couldn't figure out was why he would want to be involved. I knew what I had to gain, but I didn't know what he had to gain.

"This isn't like agreeing to go to a weekend in Cabo! This is a fake engagement." I lowered my voice. "Isn't that fraud? We could go to prison and I do not wear orange well. My skin tone is all wrong and it's a disaster."

The whole idea was making me panic. It was one thing to theorize about it, another in reality.

"You wouldn't go to prison. Fraud would be like if you paid me to pretend to be your fiancé or if we had zero intention of living together or being in a relationship."

Hold on. "Living together?" I wanted another sip of wine but my hand was trembling and I didn't trust myself not to spill it all over the table. "Why on earth would you want to do that? You barely know me. What the hell is in it for you?"

It was pure madness.

Wasn't it?

Michael took a second, like he was collecting his thoughts. I waited, heart racing.

The whole thing was absurd.

But it *would* prevent my deportation.

"I hate dating," he said. "The games, the false starts, the lack of transparency. We've talked about that. I want to be in a relationship. I want to come home to someone every night and have inside jokes and the right to put my hand on my partner's knee at a dinner party. I don't want to spend the next however long looking for that and failing. Why the hell couldn't it be us, Felicia?"

My throat felt tight, but not out of panic. It was hope rising.

"So... cut through the red tape, is that what you're saying? Just get right to it."

He nodded. "Why not? Living together, having to pretend to know everything about each other for the INS interview means we'll have a crash course in actually getting to know each other."

"What if we find out we can't stand each other?"

"It's only forty days. It's up to you how much you want to stay in New York. You can leave now or you can leave in forty days if we don't work out. Or if we do work out, you stay."

So much utter confidence.

It must be nice to have that kind of belief that you were doing the right thing. I suddenly felt like I wanted to call a psychic and ask her what the future held.

But this was not an entirely horrible idea. It was the only solution that would allow me to stay in New York.

"If I stay, we're together, then? That's it? Are we still engaged at that point or just revert back to dating?" Since the man had it all figured out.

"We stay engaged and get married before the fiancée visa expires. I'll buy you that brownstone on the Upper West Side."

Oh, God, there was a brownstone involved? Damn it. He was right. I couldn't say no to him. Thinking hard, I picked up my glass and took a sip, swishing the wine around in my mouth. What was the true downside here? There was one, maybe seven, I just needed to make sure I named them all first before I made a decision.

Who was I kidding? I'd already made my decision.

"Then we can start a family."

I almost spit the wine out. "Michael! *Children?* Have you lost your mind?"

"Don't you want children?"

That stymied me. "Well. I mean, yes. But eventually, when it makes sense. When I've got engaged and married in the proper order." Though to be honest, spending time with Savannah's baby, Sully, had been tugging on my heart strings lately. I had kind of been thinking that if and when I got married, I wouldn't mind having a baby straightaway.

But that was all theoretical.

"This is the proper order. Engaged, married, baby." Michael swirled the wine in his glass. "If you don't want to even entertain the possibility of having a baby, then I'm out."

The waitress had just reached our table but I ignored her.

"You're *out*?" I demanded, shocked.

"If you don't want a baby, yes."

The poor waitress just retreated without a word, actually backing up before turning around and heading toward the kitchen.

"Yes. I mean, we can have fun until you leave but I can't get engaged unless you agree to the possibility of children—meaning if we work out, and if we get married."

"That's a lot of ifs."

"It is. But I still want to cover my bases."

I was momentarily rendered speechless by the whole situation. My mouth kept opening and shutting like a clam.

"There isn't a lot of risk involved for you," he said. "Just a forty-day commitment."

I poured more wine from the bottle, then decided not to drink it. I needed a clear head for this conversation. "You don't think this is totally insane?"

Michael reached over and placed his hand on mine. His thumb rubbed my flesh in a gentle, arousing circle.

"Don't tell me you don't feel it. The connection between us. It's real and I don't want you to leave." His eyes were dark, his voice low, hypnotic. Sexy. "I don't want something incredible to disappear before it even starts."

He'd said there wasn't a lot of risk involved for me. But that was a complete falsehood. I could waste forty days in a disaster when I could have spent that time relocating. I could get in trouble with the government. I could get my heart broken. Because what if I wanted to stay with him and he wanted me to leave at the end of our little social experiment?

That would be bollocks. Plain and simple.

All of that.

But what did I say? "I don't want it to disappear either."

Michael pushed his chair back and reached into his pocket. He went down on a knee next to me.

A fucking knee. He was on a knee.

I heard a strangled sound come out of my mind or maybe it was my imagination. I did momentarily see black and thought I was going to pass out but it receded as quickly as it arrived.

"Felicia, will you marry me?"

A cushion cut diamond ring in a platinum setting appeared out of a box that was Tiffany blue.

"Oh fuck, oh fuck, oh fuck," was my actual answer.

I HADN'T THOUGHT a yes was a guarantee. Not at all. But I also hadn't envisioned her repeatedly saying fuck. I probably should have warned her. I had wanted a genuine reaction but this was a little too genuine.

"The waitress has my phone," I murmured, low enough that no one else could hear but her. "Documentation for an interview later."

That made her close her mouth and purse her lips in understanding before she gave me a wide-eyed nod.

"Is that a yes?" I asked, much louder.

"Yes. It's a yes."

Her hand was shaking when I put the ring on her finger. It looked good there.

The other diners erupted into applause.

She gave me a look of amazement. "Bloody hell," she said. "It's fucking beautiful."

That made me laugh. I stood up and pulled her up out of the chair. "Give me a kiss."

She did and it was hotter than I was expecting. It was like she poured all of her confusion and frustration into that kiss. I had to step back before I got hard in the restaurant. I turned, holding her hand, and smiled at the half dozen tables with diners. "Thank you. I'm a lucky man."

Felicia smiled and gave a little wave in everyone's direction. I held her hand until she was back sitting. She put her hand out and stared at the ring in awe. I actually had zero clue what she was thinking.

It had been a bold move on my part, getting that ring. But if you don't aim for the stands, you'll never hit a homerun. I'd figured if I ate the ring, so what? If we were going to pull this off, both for Immigration and for ourselves, long-term, we had to play it as if it was real.

Because my plan was that it would be real.

It didn't seem like her feelings were *exactly* the same.

But that could change. Would change. I would work my ass off to make sure of that. Why not take a crack at it and see if this turned into something amazing and long-lasting?

The waitress came over to us, beaming, handing me my phone. "Congratulations, Dr. Kincaid."

"Thank you very much. Can we get a bottle of Cristal, please? To celebrate."

"Of course."

The minute she was out of reach Felicia said under her breath, a smile plastered on her face, "I could fucking kill you now. Like literally strangle you with my bare hands."

That sounded promising. "You don't like the ring, do you? We can get a different one."

"That's hardly the issue." She was smiling in a way that should have terrified me.

Instead it turned me on.

"You don't like surprises?" I asked.

"It depends on the circumstances. I like surprise orgasms, not surprise proposals."

"Is there really any other way to propose?" I asked, settling back into my chair. "What fun would it be if the woman knew it was about to happen? Why even bother?"

She made a sound of exasperation.

"I could surprise you with an orgasm, too," I murmured. "Would that take the sting off?"

I put my hand on her knee under the table and massaged it.

Felicia bit her lip like she was trying not to smile. She shook her head slowly. "Naughty bastard."

"I warned you."

"You did. I should have taken more note."

The waitress reappeared with a bottle and popped the cork. Felicia jumped and gave a burble of laughter, as sparkly as the champagne. The initial shock seemed to have worn off.

I hadn't told anyone my plan. Not even my brother. He would think I was insane and maybe I was. But I figured it was the ultimate in speed dating. After forty days Felicia and I would either be in love and ready for a commitment. Or we wouldn't. But we wouldn't need more time than that to figure it out because it was immersion dating and we were going to learn a whole hell of a lot about each other.

"Were you serious about the brownstone?" she asked. "You can't dangle real estate in front of me and then not follow through."

"I was absolutely serious. If we get to the altar, you can pick out whatever you want. I'll keep my mouth shut about finishes and layouts and paint colors. I only reserve the right to say no if I think it's financially not a good investment."

She sipped her champagne and eyed me. "I suppose I can't argue with that. Though what are the odds it will come to that?"

It was reasonable to be skeptical.

But I felt completely confident we could make this work. "Start searching on Zillow, baby."

Felicia laughed. "God, you're insufferable."

"It's one of my charms."

"Sadly, I agree." She leaned back in her chair, crossing her leg to the side, showing me the whole length of that sexy leather boot.

"Now can we please order some food? I'm starving. My modeling days of surviving on caffeine and nicotine are over."

"You were thinner then? My God, you must have been invisible." She was already thin. I couldn't imagine her on a restricted diet.

"Yes. Fifteen pounds easily."

"The doctor in me cringes at the thought of living on caffeine and nicotine."

"It's a miracle I didn't destroy my metabolism permanently." She pulled her phone out. "Would you like to see some photos of me from the runway?"

I nodded. "Of course."

She handed me her phone and I studied the image on the screen. She was wearing some kind of giant blue garment that wrapped around her like a tube. A very skinny tube. Her hair was teased up high and her makeup was hot pink. I wasn't even sure whether it was a dress or a straightjacket. The fashion didn't interest me though. It was her expression. The classic blank stare of the runaway model. With hollow cheeks.

It didn't really reflect anything of her personality.

"Very interesting," I said. "You absolutely look the part. I can see how you were successful."

"I really wasn't that successful. But it was a learning experience, I will say that."

"I can imagine. Now since that was then and this is now, what would you like to order? Do you want an appetizer or straight to the entrée?"

The look she gave me made me very aware she was no longer thinking about dinner.

"Tonight? Straight to the entrée."

God, she was so fucking hot. I raised my hand for the waitress. I suddenly wanted to rush dinner and get her back to my place.

"So we need to establish some rules," she said, eyeing the engagement ring again.

"I agree." We couldn't just stumble into this blind. We needed ground rules. "What are yours?"

"If I'm moving in with you, all of your ex-wife's things need to go. I can't live in the shadow of her Louboutins. I don't mean to be insensitive but we'll never have a fighting chance if you're still mourning."

"Done." I didn't really want to spell out to her that my marriage hadn't been a roaring success. If it hadn't been for Becca getting sick, there was a high probability we'd have been divorced in another year. But that was a conversation for another day. "The clothes were it, really. I don't have anything personal of hers. I gave that all back to her parents years ago."

She nodded. "Okay, then. Also, I'm keeping my flat and you have no say in that."

The waitress came up to the table right then. She had pretty much the worst timing ever. Or maybe it was more like since we'd arrived, Felicia and I had been engaged in a very bizarre conversation from an outside perspective.

"Why, do you want somewhere to meet a twenty-two-year old fuckboy?" I asked Felicia. I intended it to sound casual, but it didn't. It sounded jealous, which was a dick move on my part. I should have let it go, just ordered some mussels and moved on, but the thought of her seeing another man got in my head and made my jaw clench.

Her mouth fell open. "No! There's nowhere for my stock at your place. I'm not moving all of that, for one thing. For another, I need a space to work that doesn't involve you present."

"I'm at work all day."

"I don't care."

I eyed her. I felt like we were engaged in some sort of power struggle and I wasn't sure why. "Keep your apartment. I don't care. I really don't." As long as she wasn't meeting a man there, I didn't. It made sense from a security standpoint for her, in case she decided she didn't want a K1 visa.

Or me. If she didn't want me.

"Just like that, you're giving in?"

We had to start off on the right foot or this would never work and that meant I had to fully trust what she told me was the truth. "Yes. Are you ordering or not? Anna has been standing here listening to our ridiculous conversation probably wishing we would go to hell and free up this table."

Given that Anna still didn't say anything, I figured I had the right of it.

"I'm so sorry, Anna," Felicia said. "He rattled me at fuckboy. I apologize. I'll take the branzino and whatever side you recommend with it."

"That's a whole branzino, miss," Anna said.

"I know. I'm hungry," Felicia said.

That made me grin. "Remind me not to get between you and a meal again."

I ordered the duck and sipped my wine as the waitress retreated. The champagne was too sweet for me to have more than a few sips. "Clothes gone and you want to keep your apartment. Anything else?"

"You let me have the TV remote, generally speaking."

"Now hold on a minute. What do you mean by generally speaking? Are you going to be blaring HGTV and the Food Network twenty-four/seven?"

"I don't watch Food Network. Good God, who do you think I am? I am not a woman who cooks. I do watch a lot of HGTV but I also might be a bit obsessed with crime TV. You'd be amazed how many people disappear and no one ever finds their bodies. How do you hide a whole body? It's astonishing."

I stared at her, not exactly sure if she was serious or not. "You're not watching that shit in the bedroom. You can watch it in the living room but not in bed. I'm not going to fall asleep with Deadly Women playing in the background."

She laughed. "I can see how that might be off-putting. That's fair. Keep murder out of the bedroom."

"I want that made into a neon sign for over the bed. Very modern."

"I'll get you that as an engagement gift," she said.

Felicia lifted her champagne glass and tilted it, eyeing me mischievously from under those dark lashes. It was a look that both turned me on and made me wonder what the hell I was getting myself into.

"A gift isn't necessary. Though a party probably is. For legitimacy."

Her eyebrows went up. "We can't tell people the truth, can we?"

"No. If we do, then they're culpable if they're questioned and they lie. No, we have to tell our friends it's a whirlwind engagement."

"My friends are going to figure it out. They're not stupid."

"But you can't confirm it."

She sipped from her glass, then set it down. "A holiday engagement party?"

"That works. Are you done with your demands?" They seemed simple enough. I had zero objections to what she had requested.

"We have to agree to show each other our absolute worst," she said. "If you want this to be a true litmus test. No putting on our best behavior. We have to be truthful and authentic."

I frowned at her. "I'm not sure about absolute worst. I agree with you that we should be authentic, of course. But we don't need to test each other's limits."

"I disagree. I'm going to show you all my annoying qualities so we don't get swept along with the fantasy."

I was about to grumble but agree when she raised her index finger.

"Oh, and one more thing. No sex."

SEVEN

"*WHAT?*" Michael sounded outraged. "Why? That's ridiculous."

"I don't want us to get confused by lust and attraction and think it's something more than it really is. We have to know our feelings are real if we decide to stay together after the forty days."

"We've already had sex. Great sex. You can't exactly undo that."

"Those are my rules." Or guidelines. I wasn't entirely sure I could do forty whole days without sex, giving that Michael was right. It had been great sex. "We can tonight, but once I move in, we need to show restraint."

"That makes exactly zero sense. We'll be living together. Sharing a bed. Showing our friends that we're having a relationship. People doing all of those are having sex."

"This isn't a normal relationship." The champagne was going to my head. I needed a meal or I was going to wind up believing this was a real engagement. But the bubbly tasted delicious and I couldn't seem to stop drinking it.

I was wearing a Tiffany engagement ring on my finger. It felt foreign and heavy and kept glinting in the candlelight. I was sitting across from a man I barely knew and promising to move in with him open to the possibility of both marriage and children. It was insane and I knew it was insane. And yet, I had said yes.

Ninety-nine percent of the reason I'd said yes was to give myself time to figure out a way to stay in the States. Whether that was as Michael's fiancée or for another reason entirely. But there was still one percent of me that had said yes because I wanted it to be real. Because it gave me a sliver of optimism that somehow in the end this could all sort itself out and I would have a husband.

But I had to stick with the no-sex rule because I couldn't let myself fall in love with him until I knew he was in love with me. Nor did I want to be the person who confused lust for love, which was obviously quite the common mistake. So I had to show restraint, which sucked.

"I want this to be a true test of our compatibility." I gave him a charming and possibly buzzed smile. "Please?"

He stared at me. He rolled his eyes. He swore under his breath. "Fine. But I get tonight. And I mean, *all* night. You're not going home five minutes afterward like last time."

The thought made me shiver in anticipation. I nodded. "I accept your terms."

Michael pulled a face. "How did those end up being my terms? I think I got a shit deal in these negotiations."

I put my hand over his and massaged it. "Shh. Don't worry, it will go fast. Would you like to add anything else?"

"Yes. The standard prenup contract."

That didn't bother me in the slightest. The man clearly had money, both from his career and from family. "Of course. I'm happy to sign anything."

"You have to go to the hospital's holiday party with me."

It wouldn't be my first choice of things to do, but I could manage. "Sure, not a problem." I drained my champagne. "May I have another glass?"

He lifted the bottle from the bucket and poured for me. He handed it to me and I tipped my glass back and let the smooth liquid fall down my throat.

"Sex or not, you have to show affection to me. Hugging, kissing. A lover's nickname."

I'd definitely had too much champagne because I leaned in closer to him and said, "Can I call you daddy?"

The sound he made in the back of his throat and the narrowing of his eyes showed me exactly what he thought of that.

My nipples hardened. I felt a rush of heat in my core.

My teasing had just backfired on both of us.

I COULDN'T GET Felicia back to my apartment fast enough. I basically dragged her through the lobby and waited impatiently for the elevator. Once it opened and we stepped inside, I pulled her against me and kissed her with all the pent-up passion that had been brewing while we finished dinner, the champagne, shared a tiramisu and sipped espresso.

It was debatable if she'd even wanted dessert or she was just tormenting me.

Which she was good at. No sex for almost forty days? That was bullshit.

But bullshit I was willing to endure if it meant at the end I'd have Felicia in my bed every night.

Tonight was about satiating myself to survive a month without, but also it was an opportunity to drive Felicia wild. Make her acknowledge what a hot and intense connection we had.

Her coat was covering the majority of her body, so as I kissed her I unhooked the coat's belt so I could slip my hand inside. She wrapped her arms around my neck and kissed me back eagerly, our hot breath intermingling.

Aware there were cameras monitoring the elevator, I didn't want to take it too far but I did push her against the wall and slid my hand down over her hip. I broke off the kiss and pulled back, cupping her cheeks and staring into her blue eyes.

"I want you so bad," I murmured. "You're so fucking gorgeous."

Felicia didn't say anything. But she reached out and stroked her hand across the front of my pants, easily finding my hard cock. She gave it a squeeze.

Damn.

The diamond ring I'd given her glinted on her finger. I was about to say to hell with the cameras when the door dinged and slid open. I took her hand and pulled her down the hallway. My apartment had a touch pad entry, so I punched in the code and shoved the door open. Tugging her inside, I immediately pushed her against the wall. It was harder, more urgent than I had intended, and when she gasped at impact, her eyes darkened.

"What do you think you're doing?" she asked, the corner of her mouth turning up in a smirk.

"You know exactly what I'm doing." I eased my hands inside her coat and up to her shoulders to push it down off of her. The coat pooled at her feet and ankles.

As I stripped off my overcoat and my suit jacket, I took in the sight of her. She was pressed against the wall in that tight, form-fitting dress, the black boots nearly meeting the bottom of the dress. There was a ribbon of pale skin between the two and it made me want to feel her skin, bury my hand under her dress. Kissing her hard, passionately, I gripped that exposed area of her flesh, before greedily easing up her dress.

Felicia broke off the kiss and gave a soft gasp. She reached out to hold on to my arms and arched her hips towards my touch. I absolutely loved how she never hesitated to show how turned on she was. It made me want to give her as much pleasure as possible.

As I ran my hand up her inner thigh, I reminded her, "All night, Felicia, all night."

Then I reached the apex of her thighs and groaned.

She wasn't wearing panties.

There was nothing between my flesh and her soft, warm sex.

As I slid my thumb down over her clit and sank into her wetness, I said the obvious. "You're not wearing panties."

"I like a smooth look," she said, her voice breathy, head tilted to the side.

She definitely liked the smooth look and I appreciated the hell out of that. She was silken smooth everywhere, fully waxed, and I stroked inside her tight body, knowing there was no way I was taking her to the bedroom.

I needed her here. Now.

Abruptly I pulled my hand back and she gave a cry of disappointment.

But I needed to dig in my pocket for my wallet and retrieve a condom. I undid my pants while I kissed first one corner of her mouth and then the other. She shivered and I eased her dress up further.

"That's it, daddy," she said. "Give it to me."

Never in my life would I have thought that would turn me on, but the way she looked at me, her full raspberry lips parted, her eyes bright and glassy with arousal, her nails digging into my arms, it was like a vise around my cock. The way she said it wasn't submissive or breathy or whiny. It was demanding, a power move. Which made it even hotter.

I lifted her knee up onto my hip. "Say please," I told her, teasing my cock against her clit.

She gasped and turned her head to the side. "Please," she murmured, almost as an afterthought as she enjoyed me stroking over her taut little button.

I stepped back from her, easing her leg back down, and she snapped to attention. She turned her head and gave me a look of reprimand. "Why did you stop? I said please."

"Say it like you mean it."

Felicia took a step forward off the wall, and ran her hands across my chest, smoothing my shirt. She eased the shirttail from the waistband of my pants. Then she took both sides of the shirt in a tight grip and ripped them apart. Buttons went flying. My cock got even harder.

"Please?" she said, voice low and seductive and very naughty. "Please give it to me. Daddy."

I was done. Beaten at my own game. I hauled her leg up against my hip, catching a very sexy glimpse of her black leather boots. Then I pushed her back against the wall, and thrust inside her.

We both moaned, the low cadence of mutual pleasure. Her body felt amazing, tightly wrapped around me.

I lost all sense of time, of the tightness in my calves, of the cool air around us. Hell, I lost all sense of me. I just drowned in Felicia, in the pleasure she gave me so easily, just by being her. Pounding into her, her shoulders hitting the wall each time I did, I gave myself over to the rhythm as she made the most delicious sounds of ecstasy in the back of her throat.

My balls were tight and I was so ready to explode but I tortured myself by holding back. I wanted her to come first. I brushed my palm over her nipple, before tugging down the neckline of her dress. Easing her breast out, I rolled and squeezed her nipple between my thumb and forefinger.

She gasped and I knew I was on the right track.

It only took a few seconds and she was gripping my ass with two hands and crying out in unbridled pleasure.

The sound was all it took for me to join her.

AFTER ALL THE pieces of me had shattered and somehow reassembled themselves back into a whole human, I just leaned against the wall and tried to remember how to breathe. I wasn't sure what it was about me and Michael but our chemistry was incredible. I'd never experienced anything like that, where a man could get me there so quickly with really no foreplay.

My hands were trembling as I eased off my tight grip on his ass. My legs were shaky. I was out of breath. And my whole body felt electric.

He had to practically peel me off the wall. My tit was still burst out of the top of my bra and my dress was bunched around my waist. Given I was still wearing my over-the-knee boots my toes were pinched forward in them, and my calves were burning. None of which mattered in the slightest.

"Holy fuck," Felicia." Michael rubbed his jaw with one hand and removed the condom with the other. "That was hot."

"To say the least. I don't think I can walk in these boots." I felt like a narrow reed swaying in a breeze. My equilibrium had gone to hell.

Michael ran his eyes up and down the length of me. "You're not taking them off. Not yet anyway. I absolutely one hundred percent plan to fuck you while you're naked except for those boots."

His words made a shiver run through me. I wasn't going to object to that.

"So there's only one thing to do." He reached out and scooped me up into his arms.

I laughed and wrapped my arms around his neck. "Such a problem solver. I admire that about you."

He kissed me. "One of these days your sarcasm is going to get you into trouble."

"I feel like that day is today."

"One hundred percent." Michael carried me to the bedroom and deposited me on his bed.

Had I really told him we couldn't have sex for a month? That seemed insane as I sat on the edge of the bed watching him strip fully out of his clothes.

But I had to stick to my demands because this was about stalling on my visa, not falling in love.

That was a hard concept to grasp when he stood in front of me fully naked, all hard muscles, and thick cock. He pulled me up off the bed and against him, covering my mouth with demanding kisses. He unzipped my dress and tugged it so it fell to the floor.

I'd been hopeful we would wind up back at his place so I'd chosen a black bra designed to give a boost to my cleavage. And no panties, as he'd already discovered. So it was easy for him to unhook the bra and get rid of it. Then I was in nothing but the very sexy boots. Paired with a designer dress, they were pretty smoking hot.

With nothing else on?

I felt like a porn star.

Michael clearly liked the look too. He swore and pushed me back down onto the bed.

Then he leaned in and stroked his thumbs on the spot right above where the boots ended a few inches above each knee. The soft brush of skin on skin in the cool room made me shiver. I felt deliciously exposed, raising my arms over my head, arching my back as he shifted his touch higher and higher up my thighs.

Michael's lips followed the path of his thumbs and I shifted, restless, wanting more. But he skirted my inner thighs and went to my hip, then waist. By the time he reached my breasts, both hands teasing at each nipple, I was softly moaning.

"Michael," I said, eyes drifting shut. "Please."

His body was over mine, hard and masculine and heavy, and I wanted him. All of him.

I was startled when his fingers entwined in my hair and he tugged, hard. "Look at me."

He sounded rough and dominating. I loved everything about it. Heat bloomed in my pussy and I wanted him so damn much. I stared up into his dark eyes. He had his gaze locked on me as he stroked over my clit and inside me, ensuring I was ready.

Then he lifted my leg onto his hip and replaced his finger with him. The full, thick, rock solid length of *him*.

I gave a soft cry of pleasure.

He rested, deep inside me, nostrils flaring. Then he started moving, a fast, driving pounding that had me resting the palms of my hands on the headboard as he drove me up the bed. I felt him everywhere, a commanding presence, a deep pleasure.

"How do you like being engaged?" he asked.

"I fucking love it." I punctuated the point by exploding, a shattering orgasm ripping through me. After I cried it, I asked, breathlessly, "You?"

"Best decision I ever made."

After he came, Michael fell on top of me, and I didn't even care that he was crushing me. I couldn't think, couldn't speak. I just needed to feel his weight on me, to be grounded. After a second though, he rolled off with a sigh.

"Felicia."

"Yes?" I pulled my hair out from under his shoulder, nipples still hard, legs trembling.

"You are the sexiest woman I've ever met. And I'm going to fuck you again in five minutes."

Yes. Goosebumps raced across my skin. "Thanks for the warning. I'll be sure to be up on all fours in five minutes then."

I GROANED. She was giving me a smirk that did all kinds of things to me. I pulled her on top of me as she gave a shriek of protest. "Hey."

"Hey nothing. You are going to kill me. But it will be worth it." I kissed her. "Now let me feel your skin on mine while I close my eyes for a minute. No complaining."

She didn't complain. Instead, she started shifting. Teasing. Rocking her hips against mine. There was no way I was going to relax or rest with all that action going on. She had me hard again in less than two minutes.

Gripping her hips, I flipped her off and onto her stomach.

"What are you doing?" she asked. "It hasn't been five minutes yet. Though I should have set a timer."

I stroked my hand over her tight little ass and gave her a light smack. All that creamy white flesh above those black boots was just too fucking much to resist. "I don't need the whole five minutes. Not with you being you."

Felicia rose up onto her knees. "Notice my sheer obedience here." She shifted her knees apart and put her palms on the mattress.

I swallowed. Hard. Her dark hair was cascading over her pale back and I had never wanted a woman as much.

"Duly noted," I said.

Then I grabbed her hips and joined us in hot, mutual passion.

An hour later, we were both completely depleted, and Felicia was asleep next to me, boots finally off.

All I could think was that I'd met my match.

I had just over a month to convince this amazing woman that she belonged in New York permanently. With me.

EIGHT

"DOES anyone notice anything different about me?" I asked my friends, making a point to raise my hand and rest it on my chin so the engagement ring was prominent.

"Did you get your brows threaded?" Savannah asked, sticking a plantain into a bowl of guacamole.

We were in a cute little hole-in-the-wall in Williamsburg, around the corner from Savannah's place.

"No, but I'm glad they look manicured." I fluttered my fingers. "Guess again."

"Is that a real diamond?" Leah asked, leaning across the table. "Are you testing that out before you list it?"

"Oh my God," Savannah exclaimed. "How did I miss that ring? It looks like an engagement ring."

"It is." I had to admit I was having fun with the reveal, even if it was a fake engagement.

"Did I tell you the guy I've been seeing, Ryan, has a cock piercing?" Dakota said. "I'm honestly not sure how I feel about it."

"That just seems arrogant to me," Isla said. "Like that his dick is so awesome it needs jewelry."

"Right?" Dakota shook her head. "It's supposed to be for added stimulation but I don't know. It feels like a Hail Mary pass in the fourth quarter."

They had turned the conversation and I felt monstrously disappointed. "Stop talking about dicks!"

All four of my friends eyed me like I had lost my shit. Which, I guess I had.

"I thought you just got some sex," Dakota said. "Why do you sound so angry? You should be relaxed."

I wouldn't have put it that way, exactly, but they were totally missing the point.

"Because I was trying to tell you something and you turned the subject to penis piercings." I stuck my hand out, displaying the ring. "This is not a consignment ring. This isn't for work. I am engaged to be married to Michael."

"Who the hell is Michael?" Dakota asked, tossing her blond hair back.

I wanted to do a facepalm.

"What?" Savannah screeched.

I mean, it was an actual screech. They probably heard her in New Jersey.

"I thought you just met him the other day," Leah said, sounding bewildered. "He was the group text guy, right? The one who had your iPad?"

I nodded. "Yes, I just met him in person a few days ago, but we had talked online for several weeks back in October." I made a face. "And then when he reached out to me about his wife's clothing, I responded in a DM as me."

"Wait a minute." Savannah gaped at me. "This just happened? I have a boyfriend, I can't have a profile on a dating app."

I'd given her the wrong impression. "Oh, don't worry, you don't! I deleted it ages ago. I messaged him directly. And I confessed immediately to Michael. Like, literally within five minutes of being in his flat. So he knows it was never you, but me the entire time."

"Okay, good, because that would have been fucked up."

"All of this is fucked up," was Isla's opinion. "What are you doing, Felicia?"

"Getting married?" I asked, trying to figure out what was the right tone. Playful? Crazy in love? Neither seemed very me.

"No, no one is getting married," Isla said. "Wrong answer. You can fuck him, you can date him, but you are not marrying him. Not now anyway. Talk to me about it in a year."

Exactly. "That's the plan. I have no intention of marrying him tomorrow."

Everyone seemed to give a collective sigh of relief.

Dakota shook her head. "Girl, you had me scared there for a minute."

"I am moving in with him though."

Savannah choked on her iced tea. "What?"

"That is not happening," Isla said.

I went into defensive mode, because really, hold on a second. They had some nerve judging my fake engagement. "Leah met Grant in October and she just moved in with him. That's two months."

"She knew him before that," Isla said.

"No, she didn't! He was a diner customer she waited on. She didn't *know* him."

"She has a point," Savannah conceded. "And Mad is already living with me, too."

"He was your nanny," Isla pointed out. "You've known him almost your whole life. You knew he wasn't a psycho freak."

"Michael isn't a psycho freak," I said. "He's a normal guy. A surgeon, who grew up on the Upper East Side, his parents are still married. He's charming and polite and fantastic in bed."

"He was very polite," Savannah said. "Though now I feel completely weird about the fact that I went out on a date with your fiancé."

"Don't call him that," Isla said. "This is insane."

"Michael doesn't like to date and we had an instant connection," I said. "I'm lonely and I hate dating too. Is this really so bizarre? After a month living together we're going to know if we want to be together or not."

"This is about your visa, isn't it?" Leah said, slamming her wineglass down so hard it was a shock it didn't shatter. "Javier told me your visa is expiring. In forty days. Oh, shit, Felicia! I thought you just had to renew it or something. Are you saying you have to be engaged to stay in the States?"

"What? No!" Savannah looked horrified.

Isla looked grim.

Dakota looked confused.

"I can't say anything," I said, lifting my eyebrows pointedly. "In case anyone ever asks you anything. You don't know anything. Understand?" I winked in a manner so exaggerated I probably looked like I'd been poked in the eye.

Isla swore.

Leah's mouth fell open. "I understand. But... are you sure?"

I wasn't sure which part of it she meant specifically but I nodded. "Yes, I'm sure. I have a massive crush on Michael and that hasn't changed. If anything, it's getting worse. This isn't a hardship. I really, really enjoy his company."

"I don't want you to get deported," Savannah said. Her eyes were filled with tears.

"I don't either," I said emphatically. "I didn't leave London on the best of terms last go round."

"Give me Michael's name and address," Isla said. "I'm running a background check on him."

I nodded. "That's fair."

"What do you think he did? Do you think he killed his first wife?" Dakota asked.

"Oh my God, you think he killed his wife?" Savannah looked scandalized and like she immediately believed it was the truth.

I rolled my eyes. That had totally got out of hand. "He did not kill his wife. She had cancer. That's a bit hard to fake."

"But you don't know that, do you?" Dakota asked. "You just have his word."

For a split second, they had me wondering. Then I shook my head. "No, stop. How could he get away with murdering his wife? That's absurd. Oh, and I met his brother, who also seems normal."

"I wasn't thinking murder," Isla said. "More like domestic violence charges or multiple secret lives in different states."

"That is also absurd. He's a physician, he doesn't have time to have multiple families. Again, it's fair to run a criminal background check. I fully support that before I move in with him." Though I was going to be gutted if he turned out to be a horrible human being. "Now can we all be happy for just a minute that I'm not being deported and I am having great sex with a man I find utterly charming?"

"Of course we can," Savannah said.

"I will always drink to great sex," Dakota said, lifting her margarita.

"I'm happy for you," Leah said. "You were there for me in my darkest hour when I freaked out that my relationship with Grant was moving too fast, and you were right. I was letting fear rule me and look at how happy I am now. Just because it's fast doesn't mean it's not real or right."

That touched me. "Thanks, Leah."

It was fast.

But it wasn't real.

And it might not be right.

I was doing it anyway because... what if it *was*?

"YOU'RE *MARRYING* the girl you met on a dating app who lied to you about who she was. Have you completely lost your fucking mind?" Sean demanded as we walked down Fifth Avenue together.

I had my hands shoved in my pockets because it was cold and windy, with flurries drifting around us. We were en route to our parents' apartment for dinner. "Nope. I have not lost my mind. I proposed to Felicia and she said yes."

"Of course she did, because she's psycho. She's a stalker. She has to be. A stage-five clinger. If you try to break up with her at any point, you're going to come home and find your apartment completely emptied out of all your possessions. Or worse, she'll do something like take a knife to your entire collection of suits. Or shit, what if she frames you for drugs? Has morphine stashed in your shoes or something?"

I glanced at my brother. "That is very specific. Has this happened to you before?"

"The morphine? No, of course not. I'm not a doctor. But if I wanted to exact revenge on an ex-boyfriend who was a doctor, that's totally what I would do. Pop him for drugs and get his license revoked."

"You and Felicia both watch too much crime TV. That's crazy. Also, I can see why you're single."

"Oh, great, she admitted she watches crime TV? Dude, you are so fucked. Or worse, dead. She'll marry you, kill you, and collect the insurance money."

"What happened to love at first sight? Does no one believe in that anymore?" I shook my head, more amused than angry.

"Not me, that's for damn sure."

"You're a jaded manwhore."

"You're not going to get this woman pregnant, are you? That's a lifelong commitment. You have to make sure she's not a psycho first."

"She's not pregnant." I wasn't going to comment on if I was in the future, because I didn't know the answer to that yet.

"Of course she's not pregnant yet. You just met her. Or she is pregnant but you wouldn't even know it, so you better hope that's not the case. Be safe. I'm serious."

"I will." I paused in front of my parents' building. "I'll meet you up there in a minute."

"What are you doing?" Sean looked at me suspiciously.

"Waiting for Felicia."

"You invited her up to Mom and Dad's apartment? What the hell, man? Couldn't she just meet us at the restaurant?"

"No, we're having happy hour first. That's what Dad said in his extremely clipped and Dad-like text. It would be insulting to her to have her meet us at the restaurant." I wasn't sure if Felicia would have cared or not. But I wanted to see how she was around my parents in a more informal setting instead of at dinner where sometimes the acoustics made conversation challenging.

"Did you warn them?"

"Of course I told them." I shook my head at my brother. "You're the only one who is being weird about any of this. They're totally cool with meeting Felicia."

"Do they know you're engaged?"

"Not yet."

He snorted and opened the door to the building. "This should be fun."

Felicia was actually getting out of a cab. She was wearing a thick wool coat that looked vintage to me, but I wasn't entirely sure. It went nearly to her ankles. No boots tonight, thank God. I couldn't be responsible for myself around those boots. Instead she had on conservative heels in black. It was a good meet-the-parents choice. Hopefully the dress was the same.

Though I wasn't sure what I was worried about. I didn't think my parents had much of an opinion about my dating life. I was forty-two years old, after all. They were retired, spent the winter months down in Palm Beach and had long ago given up hope of ever having grandchildren.

Felicia gave me a smile as she came over to me. "I'm very nervous," she said. "I don't meet the parents of a lot of men I've dated."

"Why is that?" I asked, giving her cheek a kiss.

"I think I've been a dirty little secret a number of times."

I really didn't like the sound of that. It made me feel like she hadn't always been treated with respect. The model who was the eye candy for some guy with a small dick and money.

"If anyone ever called you that, I hope you punched them in the gut."

She gave me a slight smile. "That's a story for another time."

I laughed. "Remind me to circle back to that." I opened the door for her. "Remember to stick as close to the truth as possible. We met on an app in October. Keep it simple. This is like a trial run for how we're going to do with the powers that be."

"Jesus, Michael, no pressure." She gave me a look of reprimand.

"Oh, and my brother thinks you're probably a psychopath who will murder me if we split up, so don't be offended if he's rude to you."

"How delightful."

We went into the elevator. "Show me your dress," I said, curious what was under that coat.

She raised a single eyebrow. "This is not the time for naughtiness."

"I just want to see it." I reached out and undid the top button. Her scarf was still covering whatever that would have revealed. "Please."

For a second I thought she was going to ignore me, but then she undid the coat and peeled her scarf off. She handed it to me to hold. Then she opened her coat, revealing a disappointingly conservative gray dress. Zero cleavage. I lowered my gaze and realized that below the thin black belt around her waist, the skirt went way below her knees. And had a killer slit on both sides. It was subtle, but it still made me want to slide my hand under it during dinner.

"Do you approve?" she asked as the elevator doors opened.

I nodded. "You look like you could be a teacher by day, a dominatrix by night."

That made her laugh. "That is not the look I was going for. I wanted conservative, but figure flattering."

"My mind went in different directions."

"Obviously."

I knocked on my parents' apartment door. It opened a few seconds later and it was my father. He was a big, blustering kind of guy. He still maintained some Irish jovialness, but he was the third generation of an immigrant family that had made serious money in tenements and running liquor and speakeasies back in the twenties. Not exactly the most moral backdrop for acquiring wealth but starting with my grandfather, the family had distanced themselves from those rough beginnings and now my father was a retired investment banker who was heavily involved in various philanthropic endeavors.

"Hey, Dad." I stuck my hand out because we were the family that shook hands and skipped the hugs. "This is Felicia Hobbs, my girlfriend. Felicia, this is Bud Kincaid. Real name Michael Edward, but Bud to everyone who matters."

"It's a pleasure to meet you," she said, offering her small hand.

He took it and drew her into the apartment with his free hand on her shoulder. "Nice to meet you, too. So you're a Brit, are you? What brought you to New York?"

"Initially, I was modeling here. Then I stayed because I just love the city."

"Dad, let us get inside before you grill her." I stepped inside behind Felicia and closed the door.

He totally ignored me. "A model, huh? Well, that's not hard to imagine. You're a beautiful woman, Felicia."

I had not expected my father to say that. He wasn't known for being a big flirt. But he was staring at Felicia in appreciation that went way beyond a casual compliment. Fantastic. I knew she was hot but I didn't need my dad to know that too.

"Let me take your coat," I said, giving my dad a glare as I stepped behind Felicia.

He shrugged like he had no idea what I was trying to convey.

My mother appeared right as I took Felicia's coat off and opened the closet to hang it up.

"What a lovely dress," she said. "Prada?"

I shut the closet door in time to see Felicia nod. "Yes, thank you. It's lovely to meet you, Mrs. Kincaid."

"Oh, call me Gloria."

My mother took Felicia by the arm and led her into the living room. They were just sitting down when my mother let out a loud exclamation. "Is that an engagement ring? That's an engagement ring! Michael, are you engaged?"

Well, fuck. I should have suggested Felicia leave the ring off so I could tell them first.

This could get messy.

My father was looking at me in astonishment. "You're engaged?"

I nodded, walking into the living room. My parents had a very traditional apartment, stuffed with antiques. Felicia was perched on the end of a divan looking at me for help.

"Yes, we're engaged," I said. "I asked Felicia to be my wife and she said yes."

My mother burst into tears.

Not exactly the response I was expecting.

NINE

I STARED at Michael's mother in alarm. Were those happy tears or was she having a meltdown over his alleged engagement? I looked to his brother, Sean, who was sitting back casually and sipping a drink. He just shrugged and looked a little smug.

Not wanting to make an enemy out of Sean even though he had accused me of being a psychopath, I gave him a polite smile and turned back to the melee. Given that Michael's mother was hugging him, I took it as a good sign and stood up to receive congratulations. Funny we'd rehearsed our relationship details but hadn't discussed whether I should wear the ring or not.

To be honest, I hadn't taken it off since he'd given it to me three days earlier. I was in love with the ring. It was gorgeous and it represented possibilities. The possibility that we might actually wind up together after all this nonsense was over. I liked sitting around in that cloud of optimism. Maybe I wanted a relationship, marriage, more than I'd thought I did.

No, that was a lie. I had known I wanted both. I had just thought they weren't going to happen for me. Nor could I allow myself to think that now.

"Come here," Gloria said to me. "Give me a hug."

I readily accepted her embrace and said, "I'm so thrilled you're happy. I know you don't know me, but I promise I'll be a good wife for Michael. He's an amazing man and I feel very lucky." My friends weren't the only ones with acting skills. I had taken a class or two back in the day when I had been modeling.

"That makes me so happy. I'd about given up on him ever getting married again. And you look young enough to have children. Do you want children?"

Sean let out a crack of laughter. "Jesus, Mom. She just walked in the door."

Gloria was holding both of my hands in hers and she had a warm, firm grip. I could see she'd been genuinely worried about her son. I felt gutted seeing the pain in her eyes.

Stick as close to the truth as possible. That's what Michael had told me.

"Yes, a family is part of the plan," I assured her, because how could I not? That was the plan. Technically. If all the stars aligned and Michael and I didn't hate each other in forty days. Thirty-seven, actually.

The number made my gut clench.

"Congratulations," Bud said. "Let's sit down and you can tell us everything."

"Yes. Sean, open a bottle of champagne so we can celebrate."

Sean rolled his eyes but he did stand and retreat into what I had to assume was the kitchen. The apartment wasn't open concept. It had elegant crown molding and was decorated in a French provincial style. It reminded me of my grandparents' house in the country. Very classy.

"So you're from England? What part?" Gloria said, once we all sat down.

"London. Specifically Knightsbridge, if you're familiar with London at all."

"Yes. I studied there for a semester in college. Knightsbridge is a lovely neighborhood."

"It is." I'd leave off for another day we'd left in disgrace, the bank practically tossing our things into the street when my father lost the townhouse.

"You do plan to stay in New York, right?" Gloria suddenly looked suspicious.

"Yes, of course."

"Felicia wants a brownstone on the Upper West Side. For starting a family," Michael said, sitting down next to me, his hand resting on my knee.

That mythical brownstone. Why did it feel like it was going to turn around and bite me in the ass? "That's not set in stone," I said, feeling the need to retreat from the potentially four-million-dollar decision.

"I'd love it if you were uptown. God, I hate going downtown. The traffic is a nightmare."

"Because it's all about you, Gloria," Bud said, looking amused.

"Oh, zip it, Bud. You know what I mean. I'm thrilled at the prospect of getting to know Felicia and planning a wedding."

A wedding. I hadn't really thought that far ahead. "We're hoping to have an engagement party before Christmas."

"How exciting! You'll have to get on top of that though. That's weeks, not months. Do you want the name of my event planner?"

"I'd love that," I said, truthfully. The thought of planning an engagement party with so little time made me break out in a cold sweat. Especially because I was also supposed to be moving into Michael's flat. "And I'd love it if you were able to help me."

The enormity of what we were attempting hit me then and I felt my cheeks grow hot. I glanced at Michael, mildly panicked.

He read my expression correctly. He gave me a smile and reached out and took my hand, squeezing reassuringly.

"I would absolutely love that. Do you have a wedding date set?"

"No," Michael said. "We just got engaged on Thursday."

"Are you expecting?" Gloria asked me, her gaze dipping to my flat stomach.

I certainly hoped not. The very idea of it gave me heart palpitations. "No."

"Not yet," Michael said.

I squeezed his hand. Hard.

Sean reappeared with several glasses and a bottle. "This is all I can find. You don't want to open this, do you?" He held it up.

It was a very expensive vintage but it looked dusty, like he'd pulled it out of the back of the wine rack.

"No, not that." Gloria stood. "Good grief, Sean. That isn't even chilled. There has to be some wine in the fridge."

This was harder than I had expected. I felt like a total fraud. Like the floor might open up and drag me to hell. Gloria was genuinely happy. It had nothing whatsoever to do with me. She just clearly wanted her son married off, but still, I felt like rubbish.

"I'd rather have a bourbon," Bud said. "Anyone else want one?"

I shook my head. "No, thank you."

Gloria came back in, Sean trailing behind her with four glasses.

"I found the bottle of wine we bought in Italy on our honeymoon. Let's open this."

"I thought you were saving that for your fiftieth anniversary," Michael said.

Fabulous. His mother wanted to pop the cork on a bottle she'd been saving for half a century to celebrate the success of her own actual, legitimate marriage? Nope. Not feeling guilty at all.

"Why wait?" Gloria beamed at us. "Is that okay with you, Bud?"

"Sure. I'll probably be dead by then anyway." He waved his hand as he poured himself a drink.

"That's only in six years, Dad," Michael said. "What's going to take you out?"

"Probably a heart attack from all that Viagra he takes," Gloria said, rolling her eyes.

"Mom!" Sean looked horrified.

I fought the urge to give a startled laugh.

"What? You'd think after forty-four years I'd have earned the right to be left alone with a good book at midnight."

Bud moved over to his wife and kissed her cheek. "Then stop being so damn sexy."

She waved him off, but she looked pleased.

Unlike Sean, Michael just looked amused, like he appreciated that his parents did still genuinely love each other.

My stomach clenched again. I had the feelings of both horror that I was lying to these people and desire for what they had. Forty-four years. It was astonishing and beautiful.

"Michael, you might want to invest in the little blue pills yourself," Bud said. "You are no spring chicken and Felicia is what, a dozen years younger than you? You need to keep her happy."

Now that made me actually laugh out loud.

It was Michael's turn to be outraged at his parents. "Wow, thanks, Dad. Way to undersell me."

Sean was also grinning. "I think it's a fair point, Mike."

"Kiss my ass, Sean."

"I'm actually fourteen years younger than Michael," I said. "But I have no complaints." I turned to him and gave him a smile, biting my lower lip. "He makes me very happy."

I meant it as a flirty innuendo but the minute the words left my lips, they sounded much weightier than I intended.

His eyes narrowed, like he heard it as well. He actually leaned in, gaze locked with mine, filled with lust and something else I couldn't define. "You make me very happy, too." He gave me a soft kiss. "I do have one complaint though," he murmured in my ear.

I knew what he meant. My no-sex rule.

I was already rethinking the damn rule. But it was the smart thing to do.

Bud uncorked the anniversary wine. He poured glasses for everyone and passed them around. He raised his glass. "To Michael and Felicia. May your blessings outnumber the shamrocks that grow."

Touched, I raised my glass to that and took a small sip.

"And to our wives and girlfriends," Bud continued. "May they never meet."

It took me a full ten seconds to get the joke. Michael was groaning. Gloria was glaring. Sean eye rolling.

But when it sank in finally, I let out a laugh because thank God for a good old Irish Dad joke when you were feeling like a hideous imposter.

"WHERE IS MICHAEL?" Leah asked me as she stood in the doorway of her old bedroom, shoving a box out of the way. "I really wanted to meet him."

I pushed my hair back and eyed the room to make sure everything was properly packed and ready for the movers who were arriving in just a few minutes. "He had a surgery he didn't want to reschedule. I can't deny some poor old woman a new hip. Besides, he paid for the movers and he would just be underfoot here. As you know, this isn't the biggest space. We can't take many more bodies."

It felt very bizarre to be leaving what had been my home and office for the last three years. Though I would be back tomorrow to work. That made it less unnerving and sad.

"Are you kidding? Remember that New Year's Eve we had twenty people in here?"

I laughed. It had been a night of sweaty bodies and laughter. "That defied physics. I still can't explain it."

"Is Javi at work?" Leah asked.

"Yes. Poor guy. He's left all alone in this place paying only a third of the rent. What an unexpected score for him." Granted, I still intended to use the other two bedrooms for work, but him not having to share a kitchen or a bathroom was a major coup in the city.

There was a knock on the door.

It was the movers. I got them organized and prepared for my whole personal life to sail out the door. It would honestly not take long. I was leaving behind my desk, desktop computer, lighting, camera, racks of stock. My bed was staying as well, to act as a sofa for me during the workday, but mostly because there was no use for a twin bed at Michael's.

The first order of business was for them to bring up everything off the truck that had been loaded at Michael's. Becca's wardrobe. I had emptied Leah's old room of my current stock just to move all of that in there easily. It was the room closest to the front door. We sat in the back on my bed, while they made swift work of the process. It only took them ten minutes to haul everything up. Then they started hauling out my belongings.

"Your organization has always amazed me," Leah said, as we sat with our legs crossed on the stripped bed.

"If I were truly organized, we would each have a coffee in our hands. Oh, and I wouldn't have failed to mail in my visa application," I said wryly.

"What's going on with that?"

"Michael and I have an appointment with a lawyer at the end of the week to start the fiancée visa process." I glanced down at my engagement ring instinctively. It was such a lovely ring. "I hope all of this is worth it in the end."

Leah gave me a look that made me uncomfortable. "Are you sure you know what you're doing?" she asked. "I'm not judging, I swear. I'm just asking. You're our dark horse when it comes to relationships. Everyone else is so predictable and you're... not."

I wasn't offended. But I also thought she was batty. "Are you joking? I go for the same type of man every single time. I'm ridiculously predictable."

"But you keep your feelings a secret. None of us ever really know how you feel."

"That's because I'm British," I said, both flippantly and truthfully.

Leah opened her mouth but I was saved from whatever she was going to say by two men coming into the room.

"We need the dresser now, miss," the one said. "I need to tip the mattress up to get it out because this room is so narrow."

"Sure." I peeled myself off of the mattress and went to stand by the window as they hoisted up the mattress. I crossed my arms and leaned against the window. "What an anticlimactic ending to our years here, Leah. You're living with your fiancé in a sprawling penthouse and I'm heading downtown. I never thought I'd live downtown."

Leah ran her hand along the wall. "This apartment truly sucks on every level. There are rats in the walls. The kitchen is a joke. The windows rattle in the winter, so its freezing, and in the summer it feels like a sauna. The water pressure is nonexistent. And the steps to the second floor of the building are not to code. They're only deep enough for size-five feet. It's a winding, rickety, deathtrap."

She was right about each and every point. "Yet, I'm going to miss it."

"Me, too," she said. "It's only been a month since I moved out but at least I've been able to come over and see you here. I doubt I'll drop by Washington Heights just to pop in on Javi. He's not a guy you pop in on."

That made me laugh. "No. He's not. I'm not supposed to talk about the whole visa thing but you should have seen Javier's face when I asked him to marry me." It was funny now. It hadn't been at the time. "He was flat-out horrified and yes, it had to do with him having a girlfriend, but it also had to do with him just being horrified at the prospect of being with me. His poker face is complete and utter shit."

"It truly is." Leah looked around. "They're really knocking out this move fast. I can drop you off at the new apartment with your suitcase and then I can go grab us some takeout while you tell them where to put stuff."

"That is a brilliant plan." Leah had her fiancé's driver waiting for us downstairs in whatever random parking spot he'd found.

"Also, you didn't get this from me, but I have some paperwork downstairs for you. It's what Immigration is looking for to prove you are a legitimate couple."

That made me start, and guiltily look down the hallways. The movers were somewhere in the exterior hallways or on the stairs. I could hear their shoes squeaking and their huffing and puffing. They'd clearly left my front door open.

"Thanks," I said. "I was scared to look any of that up on my own."

"I did it at the library. So it could have been anyone." She shrugged. "I do not under any circumstances want you to get deported and I definitely don't want you to get in trouble. I'm also one of those irritating friends who is in love and wants all of her besties to be experiencing the same thing."

"That is irritating."

Leah laughed. "I know. But seriously, just glance over it all and then pitch it in a public garbage can or dumpster. Maybe that's paranoid, but I've been watching a lot of spy shows and movies lately."

Amused, I reached out and hugged her. "You're the best and I'm very, very happy to have met you and spent years living in this shithole with you." I hooked my arm through hers and gave her another side hug. "Let's go out with style."

"Burn it down?" she asked.

"God, no! I have fifty thousand dollars' worth of merchandise in here." I grinned at her. "Oh, and Javi still lives here, remember?"

"Damn it, that's right."

"I was thinking something a little simpler." I moved out of the bedroom and down the hall. "Like this." I flipped off the apartment numbers hanging crookedly on the metal door. "Bye, 204. It's been real."

Leah raised her middle finger next to mine. "It really has been real. A little too real. Here's to never sleeping in a twin bed again."

I could get behind that. Which was why I had to figure out how to both be so real with Michael that he fell in love with me. Yet not so real that he thought I was a genuine idiot.

All without falling in love with him so I wasn't disappointed if he tossed me out.

It was a regular big old mess and I had no idea what was going to happen.

Like an online auction, I couldn't predict the outcome.

I just didn't want to be returned as "not what I was picturing."

TEN

WHEN I GOT home and pushed open the door of my apartment, I wasn't sure what to expect. Lots of boxes and a frazzled Felicia, was what I was mostly anticipating. Or Felicia busily unpacking toiletries.

What I didn't expect was to step into the Christmas display at Macy's. "What the..."

For a second I glanced back at the hallway to make sure I was in the right apartment.

Because I had left a very minimalist apartment that morning and had returned to find it had been transformed into a winter wonderland, complete with what had to be an eight-foot tree. There were empty boxes strewn around, but they were the kind that holiday decorations came in, not moving boxes. Wreaths adorned the walls of the living room and the kitchen island had some kind of glass bowl with snow inside it and reindeer. It was all classy and cheerful, but what the hell?

Felicia's head popped out from behind the back of the tree. Way higher than she was in reality, so I had to assume she was on a stepladder. "Hi!" she said brightly. "How was surgery?"

In one day I'd gone from a bachelor to a man who came home to a new décor and questions about my day. It was a hell of a shift and I didn't hate it. I was just taken aback. It was definitely intense though.

I took a cautious step forward and shut the door behind me. Had I fallen into one of her photo shoots? "Surgery went well. No issues." I kicked my snow-covered shoes off and peeled off my coat. "What... are you doing exactly?"

"Putting up the tree, of course." Her head disappeared again.

Of course. "Are you all moved in, then? I expected more boxes and a higher level of stress."

"Moving in was short work. The men you hired had it all done in two hours."

It was as I walked across my living room I realized that in addition to wreaths she had hung artwork on my wall. Art I'd never seen before. I didn't dislike it, it was just startling. There was a glass bowl on the coffee table that was new as well. I did a three-sixty and realized the whole place was like that. She had just made additions here and there. A little bit of Felicia scattered about, some holiday, some just... stuff.

All in one afternoon.

The woman was a hurricane. I was terrified to see what the hell had happened to my bathroom. She'd probably wallpapered it in a floral pattern in the course of ten minutes.

Putting my hands in my pockets I moved to the tree and searched for her among the giant branches. "Where did you get this tree?" I fingered a silver bulb. "And all these decorations?"

She glanced over at me, wrestling with some kind of ribbon. "I ordered them," she said, as if that were obvious. "They were delivered this afternoon."

"Did this need to happen today?" I asked.

Felicia looked at me like I was a complete and utter fool. "We have thirty-five days, Michael. That is it. We have to convince people we're a couple and host an engagement party. There isn't one single day to waste. In fact, you should probably help me so we can get this done faster."

I just wanted a taco and a beer after a long day and the opportunity to digest the fact that Felicia was living with me, and that it had been my idea. You know, contemplate it with some long drawn-out kisses and grinding on each other. I did not want to holiday decorate. I never wanted to do that, actually. "What's for dinner?" I asked.

She made a sound in the back of her throat. "Are you joking? It's whatever you would be eating if I weren't here. I told you I don't cook. That isn't negotiable."

"Well, I don't Christmas decorate." I reached out and eased my hand over the small of her back. "I'll order some food. Is Mexican okay?"

"Whatever you want. Why won't you help me? We could take great photos of us decorating the tree together. Some people find that sort of thing romantic."

"I'll have sex with you under the tree but I'm not decorating it."

"We can't take photos of that."

That made me grin. "Not ones we can share." I bent over and picked up a bulb and put it on a random branch.

"Oh my God, not there!" she said.

I gave her a smug look. "See? You don't even want me to decorate with you. Because you're a control freak."

Felicia jumped down off the stepstool and gave me a smile. "You are correct, sir. You're going to have to learn to live with it. I was envisioning decorating together meaning I tell you where to put things and you just do it and we post it on social media."

Fat fucking chance. That sounded really boring. "That sounds like hell to me. Is this part of your campaign to expose me to all the quirks I might not like?"

Her hair was in a ponytail and when she tilted her head to think, the ponytail swung. "Actually, no. This was me panicking when I read all the ways we can and should prove that we're an actual couple. I decided not only do we need a cozy holiday home, we need engagement photos. So please clear your schedule for two weeks from Wednesday evening at eight. I have someone swinging round. She came highly recommended."

I barely heard a damn word she was saying. All I could think was that she was absolutely beautiful and she was here. In my apartment. I shifted closer to her and cupped her cheeks. "I'll be there." Her organization, efficiency, and independence were actually hot. She might be a little neurotic and over the top, but she got the job done and I appreciated that. "You're very gorgeous when you're being a boss."

The corner of her mouth turned up. "Boss lady. That's me. Wait until you see the list I have for us. I've written a joint statement about our engagement for our social media accounts and booked us to look at six different wedding venues so it appears we're genuinely searching for a site."

"Just tell me where to be and what to do." I closed in on her and kissed her, breathing in her scent. Her lips were soft beneath mine. I had exactly zero intention of going to look at six venues, but I would break that to her later. When she saw the control freak side of *my* personality.

Right now I just wanted to taste her. Enjoy her presence. Talk her into sex. My hands slipped down to squeeze her firm ass in her leggings.

She sighed against me, kissing me back, eagerly. Her hands went around my neck, but then she pulled back. "No. Don't distract me."

"I was just saying hello to my fiancée."

"Beast. Go order your food. We can eat and go over my list."

I shook my head but said, "Can't wait. What do you want if I order Mexican?"

"Fish tacos." She stepped back up on the ladder and went back to her decorating. "The list is on the island. We'll burn it after we go through it."

That made me laugh. "Excellent. Burn the evidence."

I wasn't laughing when I sat down on the sofa with her twenty minutes later, tacos on a plate in front of me, and looked at the list she had. It was daunting. "I'm really supposed to know all these things about you? What celebrity makes you want to scream? Why would I know that?"

Felicia sat next to me and dipped a pepper into the guacamole. "Harry Styles. I'm sure he's a great guy and he has a lovely voice. But his tattoos are too random. It frightens me."

That made me shake my head. "Okay, so now I know two things about you. You are bothered by both Harry Styles and random tattoos. Got it."

"What celebrity bothers you?" she asked, biting her pepper.

That was easy. "Any celebrity who spouts medical advice when they have zero medical education or training."

"That makes sense."

"I'm glad you approve of my answer," I said, amused. I went back to the list. "Do you think mermaids exist? Felicia, the person interviewing us for your fiancée visa is not going to ask if you believe in mermaids. I can guarantee it."

"You can't guarantee anything," she said, going back to the guacamole with the second half of her pepper.

"You're double dipping," I pointed out.

"I turned it around. I didn't put the end I bit back in."

"That's still double dipping."

Felicia gave me a look. She took another pepper and drew it into her mouth, sliding it in and out. She flicked her tongue over the tip while I instantly got hard. In and out that pepper went, while she licked and sucked. Her eyes were filled with mischief.

She knew exactly what she was doing to me and she was doing a damn good job making me envious of a pepper.

Then she stuck the pepper into the guacamole.

"What the hell was that?" I asked, reaching for my beer. I needed something to cool me down after her little blow job simulation.

"I licked it, so it's mine," she said. "Now I don't have to worry about double dipping. It's all mine since you're so worried about what's been in my mouth."

Damn. "Put whatever you want in your mouth. I take it all back. Lick and suck whatever you want."

"What about biting?" The corner of her mouth turned up.

I picked up my taco before I broke her no-sex rule on the very first night living together. "Only I get to bite."

She laughed. "Typical. Now keep reading that list. We're basically down to thirty-four days now. The day is almost over."

"Can't we just enjoy our dinner and your beautiful Christmas tree?" I had to admit I liked the way the white lights were twinkling and casting the room in a soft glow.

"We don't have time to enjoy anything."

That made me laugh. "Five minutes. That's all I'm asking for." I picked up my taco and gestured to the tree. "I told you I haven't decorated for Christmas in a decade. It's nice. It feels homey in here. You did a good job."

"Thank you. I actually enjoyed it. The space is easy to work with. It would be even more fun if I'd had more time to do it. We can finish up after dinner."

I saw the way she slipped that in. "I have work to do," I said, lying.

She rolled her eyes. "Then we really need to get back to the list. Facts, Michael, we need to have facts to give these people."

For a woman who had thought this whole idea was insane, she seemed very motivated to make it work, which made me pleased. I wanted this to work with Felicia. I wanted to go the distance with her, which might sound fucking crazy. But I was a man who went with his gut and I knew I wanted her. "Ask me anything you want to know."

"What is your favorite scent or aroma?"

"You."

Felicia laughed. "That is a bizarre thing to say. No. You need to answer something like lavender or cinnamon or the scent of the ocean."

"Is this how our marriage is going to be? You ask me a question, I give my opinion, and you tell me my answer is wrong?" I wasn't annoyed at all. I was finding the whole conversation and her intensity surrounding it entertaining.

"I'm just saying that your answer is not what they're going to be looking for. They can't ask me what your favorite scent is and I answer 'Oh, his favorite thing to smell is me.' We'll look mad."

I would play along. "Fine. I like the smell of coconut."

Felicia made a face and reached for her plate. "Well, that's an odd choice."

I laughed. "Seriously? What is your favorite scent?"

"Chanel No. 5. It reminds me of being a child and climbing all over my mother's lap while she got ready to go out. It reminds me of trying on her pearls and putting on her lipstick."

"Your mother went out frequently?"

"All the time." She bit her taco, then licked her finger.

Even that turned me on. I wasn't going to survive thirty-four days without being able to take her.

"My mother went out to lots of lunches and fundraising events," I said. "It all seemed boring as hell to me as a kid, but now I understand she was actually working damn hard being philanthropic."

"Oh, my mother wasn't charitable. She was a socialite. She loved her parties."

"What about you?" I asked her. "Do you love your parties?"

"Not at all. I left my club days behind in Milan. Being a model there I had VIP access, and I have to admit, that was fun. But when I got back to New York, I was a regular old nobody who had to wait in line. It took some of the thrill out of it." She eyed me. "Were you one of those frat bros Americans talk about?"

I nodded. "I was in a frat, yes. Though I wouldn't call myself a bro, I did like a good keg party back a hundred years ago. There is nothing wrong with that, you know. It's a rite of passage to party at college. I was the king of beer pong." While maintaining a four point oh GPA, but I didn't want to brag.

"Were you popular with the girls?" she asked, looking amused.

"Of course," I said. "I was a fucking catch." That wasn't exactly true. I had done all right but I wasn't taking home a different girl every night. That had never been my style.

"Modest too. What if they ask me what you studied at uni?"

"I majored in biology and bio engineering. But they're not going to want details. Besides, just tell them you were eight when I was in college."

She laughed. "That sounds horrid. And truthfully, I was more like six."

"Thanks for pointing that out. If you call me daddy again, I can't promise you I won't do whatever it takes to make you stop." Just the thought made me want to push her down onto the couch and distract her with my tongue.

"Oh, tempting," she said. "But I will behave. For now."

Damn. "That's disappointing."

"I'll make it up to you later."

I really, really hoped so. I squeezed her knee and looked at Felicia. Why did she fascinate me so much? I wasn't sure, but she had me totally wrapped around her finger.

"WE NEED to know each other's toothpaste brands. That has to be in the interview."

Michael was wearing flannel pajama pants and a soft T-shirt and looking quite domestic and adorable. It was going to be hell to be snuggling up against his muscular body in bed and not have sex. But I had to keep some kind of boundary in place or I'd fall madly in love and then if it didn't work out, I'd be both tossed out of the States and devastated with a broken heart. No, thank you.

"Why would that be in the interview?"

"Because it was in The Proposal."

His eyebrows rose as he came up to the sink next to me. "You think a movie has accurate information on immigration interviews? And I don't remember that being in The Proposal anyway." He shook his head. "But fine. This is an easy one. What toothpaste do you use?"

He picked up my tube. "What is this? Macleans. I've never heard of it."

I snatched it back. "It's British. I'm very brand loyal."

He'd already lost interest. His hand came up and his finger strolled along the neckline of my nightgown. "I like this."

"You need to tell me your toothpaste brand," I said, determined to keep him on track. And him giving me that look was not helping my resolve to abstain from sex.

"Crest." He was totally in my personal space. "Do you wear these silky things every night?" His finger ran down over my nipple and down my abdomen.

I nodded. "Cotton gets twisted. I can't stand to sleep in pants either."

"This is very sexy."

I held my toothbrush up between us, preventing him from kissing me. "Brush your teeth, Michael."

He groaned, but he obeyed. "Fine. It has been a long day."

It had. I had shifted my entire life in twelve hours.

We brushed in our separate side-by-side sinks. It felt oddly intimate. I didn't really know Michael all that well. I didn't want him to see me spit. Yet we were engaged. The thought made me finish up quickly and go get in the big fluffy bed. It was cold in the room and I snuggled under the thick blankets.

"That's my side," he said when he entered the bedroom. "Scoot over."

He actually patted my butt and kind of shoved me across the mattress.

"What the hell? You could have given me two seconds to move."

"This was easier." He spooned me and sighed as he relaxed.

I stared at the windows of his bedroom and blinked against the harshness of the overhead chandelier. "You do realize the light is still on."

"Shit. Can you turn it off?"

"No! I was in bed first. The last person in turns out the light. Everyone knows that rule."

"But you're closer to the door."

"Because you shoved me over like I was a cat in your bed." I wasn't getting up. It was December, it was snowing again, and my feet were cold.

He made a sound that might have been an agreement or a protest, I couldn't tell.

"Michael, turn the light off."

I waited, then realized the bastard was asleep. "Seriously?" I asked.

To which, of course, I got no response. I wasn't getting up to turn the light off. Hell no. He needed to be trained. It was called *fairness.* Last one in turned off the light and I would die on that hill, proving that point.

Or sleep with the light on to prove my point.

I actually did that. It was a hellish, miserable night of sleep, but I did it. I tossed and turned, but I stubbornly refused to get up and put out the light and finally I settled into a restless sleep with the blanket mostly over my face.

IN THE MORNING, I vaguely heard my alarm going off. I turned it off, and tried to fall back asleep, not even sure why I had set it. Then I remembered why I'd set it. Because I had to commute to Washington Heights now that I was living with Michael. I needed to get ready and take the train, as opposed to stumbling down the hall for coffee and then straight to my computer.

This officially sucked.

My alarm went off again.

I pried my eyes open to find my phone screen and the harshness of the overhead light hit me in the eyes. Right. We'd slept with the lights on.

As I fumbled around, I actually knocked the phone off the

nightstand where it continued to squawk. I ignored it, stiff and groggy.

"Felicia. Shut that alarm off," Michael said, sounding sleepy.

"I can't. My phone fell on the floor."

"So get it off the floor." He shifted in the bed, rolling over. "Oh my God, why is the light on? What time is it?"

"It's five thirty. The light is on because you wouldn't turn it off last night."

"Are you kidding me?" He groaned. "Make it stop. My ears are bleeding."

"You get it. That makes about as much sense as me turning the light off when you got in bed last." The alarm really was irritating but I was stubborn and the air was freezing cold. We needed to talk about the thermostat setting.

"Fuck." Michael threw back the covers, burying me in them.

Even drowning in blankets, I was aware that he flicked the light off. "You turn the light off *now*? What is even the point?"

He didn't answer. I watched him stumble around the foot of the bed and bend over to get my phone. He turned off the alarm, which was a relief, I had to admit. He tossed the phone on the nightstand carelessly.

"Be careful, you'll break my screen."

"I'll buy you a new one."

I was about to reprimand him when he climbed back into bed and lay on top of me like I wasn't even there. "Michael, get off of me!"

"No. You're very cozy." He nuzzled his head into my chest.

I laughed, shoving at him. "Stop. You're crushing me. Is this what marriage to you is like, you take the whole bed? This isn't selling it."

"What's yours is mine." He gave me a sleepy and ridiculously charming smile. "I like being close to you."

"My lungs are collapsing."

"Obviously not, because you're still talking." But he did roll off of me. "Why are we up so early?"

"Because I have to get dressed and commute to work now. I want to be there by eight. That's my normal start time."

"You need two and a half hours to get to Washington Heights?"

"Pretty much. I need a shower, to get dressed, grab coffee, take the train." I flung the covers off of me. "I'll see you tonight. By the way, I think we need an app that allows us to turn the heat down at night, but then turns back up at like five in the morning. It's bloody cold in this room."

Michael rolled over and watched me, paying particular attention to my chest. "I can tell."

He reached out and touched my taut nipple. I slapped his hand. "Down. Have a good day." I gave him a kiss, despite being a little concerned about bad breath.

He tried to take more kisses and to hold me in the bed, but I wiggled free. By the time I got out of the shower, he was sleeping again. So Michael was not a morning person. I made a mental note of that.

As I stepped outside in the brisk morning air, the street still dark, I shivered beneath my puffer coat. How long until my lease with Javier was up? Five and a half months. I was either going to be back in London by then or I would still be with Michael, in which case I needed an office closer to SoHo. There was nothing fun about being in the cold in the dark, crowded on the train. I was officially spoiled.

Once I got off the train, I still had a ten-minute walk, so I checked the time. It wasn't even seven thirty yet. I figured the only one of my friends who might be awake would be Savannah. I shot her a text. *You up? Can you chat?*

Sure, just feeding the baby.

I hit call and put my headphones in my ears.

"Hi!" she said, sounding very cheerful for so early in the morning. "How are you?"

"Feeling very pissy and like a straight-up diva. How do people commute every day? It's freezing and early and my coffee got cold after two stops on the train."

"Get coffee when you get off the train. I agree, though. Commuting is not fun. We're very fortunate."

"I'm a recluse, but that's better than this."

"How was your first night living with the good doctor?"

"We slept with the bedroom light on because we were both too stubborn to get out of bed and turn it off, so we're off to a rousing start."

Savannah laughed. "That is ridiculous."

"I realize that." I buried my hands deeper into my pockets. "I also realize that given half a chance, I might fall in love with Michael."

"Isn't that the point?"

"No! Of course not, are you mad? If I fall in love with him, I'd be gutted if he dumps me in thirty-four days. Besides, I have a terrible track record picking men."

"Welcome to the club. I didn't pick Maddox so much as he picked me. I was too stupid to see what was right in front of me."

"But you knew Maddox was a good man. You've known him for years." Was there anything cuter than a friends-to-lovers scenario?

"And sometimes its love at first sight."

That made me uncomfortable because it implied I was already in love with Michael. "He did not fall in love with me at first sight," I said, because deflection when you're already emotional is a wise move. I rolled my eyes at myself.

"I wasn't there, so I don't know. But I do know that he asked you to marry him about a minute later."

"Because I'm being thrown out of the country."

Savannah believed in love wholeheartedly. I could practically see her waving her hand in dismissal. "Details. He moved you into his apartment. That's huge. I think you're going to stick, you and Michael, and I think it's *adorable*."

"Adorable is not the word I would use. Twisted might be better. I mean, can you imagine telling children this story? Yes, children, Mummy catfished Daddy and then was about to be deported so Daddy proposed. Such a charming story."

"Being sarcastic is just a defense mechanism."

"I readily admit that. Now, how are you? How is the baby and your tatted and muscular boyfriend?"

I listened to her chatter away about how happy she was and how Sully had popped out another tooth. It all sounded so lovely and ordinary. I wouldn't mind having a bit of that for myself.

"Oh, gotta go," she said abruptly. "We have a diaper accident."

"Sure thing, I'll chat with you later."

After she ended the call, I rounded the corner and saw my building.

Funny how it looked different first thing in the morning.

What else was going to look different when I turned a corner?

ELEVEN

"THAT WAS YOUR LAST PATIENT," Sara, the RN who worked with me, said.

"Thank God. I need a coffee the size of my head."

"You're really dragging today, Dr. Kincaid," Sara said. "You're not getting sick, are you?"

"He has a new girlfriend," Kim said, as she sailed down the hallway, a stack of folders in her hand. She gave us a grin. "Late nights, right, Dr. K?"

It was both true and sadly false. I wasn't worn out from sex. I was tired from Felicia's alarm going off at the crack of ass. I wasn't about to admit that. "I plead the fifth."

That only made it worse. They both laughed. "Oh, la, la," Sara said. "What's her name?"

"Felicia."

"Do you have a picture?"

It had to come out sooner or later, so I pulled my phone out of my pocket. I scrolled until I found the photos from the night we'd gotten engaged. We'd taken some selfies. I picked one and turned to show it to Felicia.

"Wow, she's beautiful."

I had to admit, looking at the picture that one, she was beautiful. Two, I was lucky she was even giving me the time of day. "She is." I gave Sara and Kim a look. "Before you comment, yes, she is fourteen years younger than me."

Kim laughed. "Don't be paranoid. No one cares about that anymore. Unless it's a woman dating a younger man."

"Sadly, that is true. If either one of you wants to date a younger man, I fully support you in doing so." I flipped through the pics, trying to find a different one I liked. I really did need to post something online. Felicia had sent me a statement to post but it had read like she wrote it, which she had. I needed something that sounded more genuinely like me.

"How did you meet?" Kim asked.

"Hold on!" Sara pointed to my phone. "Is that you *proposing*?"

It was and it was super obvious. The whole "down on one knee" was a dead giveaway. I guess there was no point in denying it. "Yes. Last Thursday night. She moved in with me yesterday."

They both stared at me in astonishment.

"You keep things close to the cuff, geez," Sara said. "I tell you about every single date I go on."

"It was quick but when you know, you know." I shrugged.

"Well, congratulations," Sara said. "I'm happy for you. You need some love from a lady."

That made me wince. "What the hell, Sara? What does that even mean?" I held up my hand. "Don't answer that."

"This is so exciting," Kim said, though she sounded skeptical. "Have you set a date?"

"No, not yet. Or I don't think so. Felicia is kind of a bulldozer, so for all I know she's set a date and booked a venue already. I do know she is planning an engagement party before Christmas, so I'll keep you posted."

"Before Christmas? That's less than three weeks away."

"I know. But she and my mother are working together, so I have total confidence they'll bully it into happening." I put my phone in my pocket. "I have to head out. I have an appointment. See you tomorrow."

They waved and we said our goodbyes. I went to my office to grab my coat. I had to meet Felicia at the lawyer's office.

I got there forty minutes later and the receptionist ushered me inside. Felicia was already sitting in front of a large desk. The attorney was around my age and he stood up to shake my hand. "It's a pleasure to meet you. Thanks for offering us some advice on how to proceed with a fiancée visa for Felicia."

"I'm happy to help."

The lawyer's name was Ken and he had the smooth, calm demeanor of someone who dealt with people in dire straits all day long. "Tell me a little bit about your situation."

I looked at Felicia. "You can tell him, sweetheart."

She made a face but she said, "I'm British. I have a temporary visa but it's expiring next month. Michael and I are engaged and we want to apply for a fiancée visa until I can get a permanent spousal visa."

"As you're probably aware, there has been a crack down on visas. So I'm glad you came to me before your visa expires. Once that happens, it's difficult to backtrack. What type of visa are you on?"

Felicia crossed and uncrossed her leg. "Well. In the past I've been on a student visa and then a temporary work visa. This was a visitor visa with a B1 extension."

That was news to me. She *lived* in New York, had a lease and a business. How long was a visitor visa?

The lawyer stared at her. "I see."

That didn't sound good. "How do we start the application process?"

"We can start the process today but be prepared for it to be denied. Felicia has been granted more visas than we generally see and applying for another may raise some red flags."

I looked at Felicia.

She gave me an innocent look that didn't look innocent at all.

"Are you working right now?" he asked her.

Felicia cleared her throat. "I sell vintage clothing online. But my business is incorporated in the UK."

"I see," he said again. "Are you both willing to proceed even with the possibility it will be denied?"

I nodded. "Of course."

"Are you aware, Dr. Kincaid, that you are accepting financial responsibility for Felicia for a period of ten years, whether you remain married or not, as long as she stays in the United States?"

I did not know that, but it didn't matter. As if I were going to let her be homeless if we didn't work out. Not that she would be. Felicia had a certain hustle to her. She was a successful business-woman all on her own. "I have no issue signing off on that. And please, call me Michael."

"So what are my chances of success here?" Felicia asked.

"I can't really say. But trust me, there is no guarantee."

Felicia gave me a worried look.

"It's okay," I told her, squeezing her knee. "It will work out."

"Either that or it's my last New Year's Eve in New York."

That sounded ominous. "Think positive."

We filled out all the paperwork and I paid the lawyer a ridiculous amount of money, then we left together.

When we got downstairs, Felicia said, "Are you sure you want to do this? I have this feeling I'm not going to get approved."

"You don't know that."

"But it's not a guarantee." She pulled her coat close together over her chest. "This could be a massive waste of time. I thought the odds were better. I don't want to hold you to this, Michael."

I stared at her, not sure if she was feeling guilty or hopeless or both. "Are you looking for an out? Is this not what you want?"

"What I want is irrelevant. I'm the massive idiot who got myself into this." She held out her hand and stared down at the engagement ring I'd given her. "I just don't want to waste your time," she repeated.

"Spending time with you would never be a waste," I said, and I meant that. "Now let's walk, it's freezing out here."

I put my hand on the small of her back and guided her down the sidewalk. I bent over to murmur in her ear, "You don't get it, do you? I fell for you before I even met you in person. I'll fight to keep you here. I'll fight to keep you with me."

She glanced up at me, her blue eyes displaying vulnerability.

I couldn't even begin to say that I knew what Felicia was thinking. Now, or half the time. She was an enigma, but I enjoyed every minute with her. I didn't want her to leave New York.

I didn't want her to leave me.

"Then you're just as massive an idiot as I am," she said.

That made me laugh. "I guess so."

"DON'T BE ANGRY," I said out loud to Becca's ghost. "I know a woman's closet is sacred, but I have to keep some clothes here at Michael's flat."

The closet bothered me and I didn't even know why. It wasn't like I felt a presence of someone. Of Becca. Because I didn't. It was actually just a hushed room that had the feel of a space that hasn't been used in years. It had needed a massive dusting when the movers had taken Becca's clothes out, so now I was finally unpacking while Michael was at the hospital.

I didn't have Becca's volume of clothing and shoes.

My wardrobe looked sparse compared to the space that existed.

"You had great taste," I assured Becca. "Though we do have slightly different tastes. Sort of like relationships, you know. I wonder if I'm quite different from you. I expect that I am."

Something about talking to her made me feel less intimidated. I wasn't sure if I was intimidated by the memory of Becca or intimidated by the weight of expectation I felt from Michael. He'd been too nice at the lawyer's. He should have been angry and the fact that he hadn't been made me nervous.

"Michael is a man who gets what he wants, isn't he?" I asked, as I pulled open a drawer and started unpacking my necklaces, bracelets, and watches. "Did you have a whirlwind romance? It makes me wonder. I have a hard time picturing him being patient if he'd decided he wanted to be with you."

This was the nicest closet I'd had since we'd left the Knightsbridge townhome when I was sixteen. "Michael did say we'll move if my visa gets approved, so I won't be here long, squatting in your closet. Unless you don't mind, in which case give me a sign."

My phone rang, making me jump. "Shit, that scared me." It was Isla.

I thought about not answering it, because I was afraid she was going to tell me Michael was a murderer, but then I realized it would really be wise to know if he was.

"Hello?"

"Hey, what are you doing?"

"Unpacking. Becca's closet feels like hallowed ground I'm treading on."

"Does Michael make you feel that way?"

"No, it's all in my head. But I feel like I'm taking over her life. Sort of like the Daphne du Maurier novel Rebecca." I gasped. "Oh my God, Rebecca. Becca. The first wife. That makes me the second Mrs. DeWinters. The second Mrs. Kincaid. The one with the very short courtship."

"What the hell are you talking about?" Isla asked. "I read it in high school and it was all moody and gothic. Your life isn't gothic."

I caught sight of myself in the mirror. "Tragic is more like it if you saw my hair and outfit right now. No wonder I feel intimidated by a dead woman's closet. I'm a fright." My hair was up, I had no makeup on, and I was wearing leggings and an enormous sweatshirt.

"I have to tell you that I did not find any evidence that Michael killed Becca. She had a rare form of breast cancer that women in their twenties and thirties get. I found her obituary and a fundraiser honoring her."

"You sound disappointed." I stopped eyeing myself in the mirror. "I never doubted she actually had cancer. And I can't exactly say 'glad to hear it,' Isla. That would be horrid."

"I was just making sure. He also doesn't have a criminal background and I did find his med school class photo and it's him, so no false identity."

"Have you thought about becoming a private investigator? You seem to enjoy this sort of thing."

"I'm not going to lie. I actually did enjoy it. I'm doing this with every guy we all date moving forward."

"You do that." I laid out a pair of chandelier earrings in one of the drawers.

"Rebecca and Michael got married three months after their engagement. Keep that in mind. He might want to rush you to the altar."

I wasn't sure how I felt about what she'd said. I wanted to feel like Michael wanted me, not just any warm body for a wife. Maybe he was just decisive. "Duly noted. Though there won't be any chance for him to marry me if I don't get approved for the visa."

My phone beeped. I pulled it back and saw it was Gloria, Michael's mom. "Isla, I've got to run. Michael's mother is on the other line."

"Sure. Remember we have drinks on Friday."

"I'll be there." I shifted my phone and answered the call. "Hello, Gloria, how nice to hear from you."

"Hi, Felicia, how are you?"

"Great thanks. And you?"

"I'm fine. Just wondering if you're free for lunch tomorrow. We can go over the details for the party."

My work schedule was really taking a back seat but it wasn't like I had a choice. There would be a hell of an interruption to my career if I had to go back to the UK. "Of course. Just tell me when and where. I'll be in Washington Heights in the morning."

"Do you mind coming down here? I'll text you a restaurant."

"Not at all." There really wasn't any reason for me to inconvenience Gloria. I would just come back to Michael's, then, after lunch.

"Thank you, dear, I'll see you tomorrow."

We ended the call and I turned to pull my favorite Versace dress out of the wardrobe box I had yet to unpack. "Becca, did you get on with Gloria? This second-wife thing is dicey."

"Felicia?"

I started. Michael had come home without me realizing. Fortunately, he was still in the living room. It might be a little unnerving for a man to hear his nearly total stranger fiancée chatting up his dead first wife.

"I'm in the closet," I called out.

He appeared in the doorway, still wearing a suit from being at work. It was sexy as hell. He was sexy as hell. He peeled his jacket off. "Hey. I didn't realize you weren't done unpacking."

"Almost finished." I tried to be casual but I was dying to ask him more about his marriage. "Being in here makes me think of Becca... how did the two of you meet?" I wasn't looking at him, but was hanging up dresses.

For a second he didn't respond. Then he just said, "We met through friends at a party."

"How long did you date before you got engaged?" That was me, being super casual. Not.

"A couple of months, I don't remember exactly."

Michael shifted in behind me, startling me. His hands ran down the length of my arms. He kissed the side of my neck. "Why are you asking me about Becca? Are you feeling jealous?"

"What? Of course not. I'm just curious." More worried than jealous. What if Isla was right and Michael was just a man who snagged a woman, regardless of who she was?

Though that didn't really make sense given he'd been single for a decade.

I continued to fuss with the sleeve of a dress and didn't turn around.

"Becca was a wonderful woman in a lot of ways. But she was also frivolous and demanding."

I closed my eyes and didn't respond, feeling emotionally overwhelmed and I wasn't sure why. Too many changes in a short period of time, that's what it had to be.

"Our marriage was actually on the rocks when she got sick. I felt guilty about that, you know. It's probably part of why I didn't date for the first few years."

That made me open my eyes. "I'm sorry to hear that. You shouldn't feel guilty. Neither of you could have predicted she'd get sick." I turned around. "Do you need a hug?"

The corner of his mouth turned up. "I need a lot of things. But I'll definitely take a hug."

I wrapped my arms around him and rested my head on his chest. I gave him a squeeze. I liked the way he felt, strong and muscular. I pulled back and gave him a stern look. "See, that is exactly why I told you we have to be totally honest about our flaws. We don't have that much time to get to know each other and you need to be really sure you want to move forward with this engagement."

"I am being totally honest with you. I'm a sexually demanding man who hates mornings."

That made me laugh. "Who leaves beard hair in the sink after shaving."

"Exactly. But I can just be a real dick if that would make you feel better."

I rolled my eyes and dropped my arms. "Absolutely. I'd love that. Now let me get changed so we can take more pictures. Immigration is looking to see that we have a history together."

"We don't have a history together."

"That's why we're going to change outfits and take selfies in various places."

Michael tossed his jacket on the ottoman in the center of the closet. "You're joking. Please tell me you're joking."

"I'm not joking. Didn't you read the list? I'm making a scrapbook. I'm dating it back to late September so we'll have to do some shots outside with just T-shirts."

He opened his mouth like he was going to tell me I was

bonkers, but then he just shook his head and closed it again. "Whatever you want, sweetheart."

"Get out, then, so I can change."

"I'm fine. You can change now." He stood there and gave me a grin.

"No, I don't trust you!" I shoved him. "Out."

I was very tempted to say to hell with my rules and let him take me against the wall.

Given the smirk on his face he knew it.

I pushed him again. He groaned but he left.

I locked the closet door behind him. Just in case.

TWELVE

EVEN THOUGH I was freezing my ass off in a T-shirt when it was twenty-five degrees to make it look like we were posing in September, I wasn't angry about it. Felicia's determination and tunnel vision were a force to reckon with and I wasn't going to slow her down. If she was willing to do all this, she had to be willing to marry me, right?

That was my working theory and I was running with it.

Because I wanted Felicia to be my wife and I would do whatever it took to convince her.

"Try not to look like you're shivering," she said as we posed with street hot dogs.

I was pretty sure our breath was going to be captured as a vapor cloud when we took the picture but I just smiled and went along with it. Everyone around us was bundled up in coats, there were Christmas lights everywhere, and it was dark outside. I wasn't sure how any of this was going to look like September, but maybe she intended to crop it in really close.

"I'm not eating this hot dog," I told her. "You've already had us posing with ice cream, coffee, and sushi. I had one too many California rolls."

"I'm not eating it either." After she took about six photos, she turned and handed the hot dog to a man who was sitting in a doorway, cardboard laid out over top of him, clearly down on his luck.

For a second he looked at her suspiciously, like she might be trying to poison him, but she smiled and said, "Happy Christmas."

"Thanks, you too." He took a bite and his face lit up. "That's a good dog."

"Here." I gave her my hot dog. "Give this to someone else. You're less intimidating than if I approach someone." I didn't want to make anyone feel uncomfortable and having a guy lean down into your space could be perceived as threatening. Besides, Felicia had a warm smile that people responded to. She was compassionate and that was something I appreciated.

She smiled at a woman who appeared to be pacing back and forth for warmth. This lady gave her a hug after Felicia handed her the hot dog, and Felicia returned the embrace without hesitation. It made my heart feel like a fist was wrapped around it.

Felicia was a complicated and layered woman and I was eager to see all her sides. There was a lot she hadn't yet told me about herself. She didn't talk about her past relationships and I wondered why. Hell, maybe it was as simple as just because I'd never really asked her.

But right now, I was just going to enjoy her quirky juxtaposition of fake photographer paired with compassionate human.

"I just had an idea!" she said as she came back over to me. "We need a picture of you carrying me on your back."

"What? Why?"

The woman she'd given the hot dog to had followed her.

"This is Linda," Felicia said. "She's going to take the picture for us."

"It's nice to meet you, Linda."

The woman nodded and chewed.

I didn't really want to pose for a picture with Felicia on my back because that seemed a little over the top. But I also wanted to eventually have sex with her again, so I was willing to toe the line.

"Can I put my sweatshirt back on at least? Parts of my body are freezing that I don't want frozen."

Linda cackled. Felicia did not. At least Linda got my sense of humor. Felicia was choosing to ignore my innuendo.

"Yes, you can put your sweatshirt back on. Hurry, though, we haven't got all night."

That made me roll my eyes. Now she had a time frame on our fake photos? "Sure, babe. Whatever you say."

I pulled my sweatshirt on and turned so Felicia could jump onto my back. Her jump was poorly timed and she just collided with my back. Then she couldn't seem to get enough height to get up. I was bent over and she was just grappling at me and getting nowhere.

"What is going on back there?" I asked, amused.

"Stupid skinny jeans. I can't get my legs apart."

"I can get your legs apart."

Linda laughed again. Linda was okay in my book.

"Don't be gross. Just bend down lower."

I was practically in a full squat but I obediently went lower. I was going to point out later what a good fucking sport I was. Felicia launched herself onto my back. Thank God she weighed next to nothing. I reached back and grabbed a hold of her thighs and hitched her higher up into place. Then I stood back up.

The last time I'd had a woman on my back was probably med school. I felt absolutely ridiculous. I also felt like I would do anything for Felicia. She was clinging to me and making little sounds of both distress and amusement. I liked the feel of her draped across my back, her hair falling over my shoulder.

Digging in my pocket, I got out my phone and handed it to Linda. She took a couple of pictures and returned it to me, without any annoying instructions on how to pose. Linda was going to get a tip from me because she was all right and being a good sport. "Thanks, Linda. Have a nice night." I slipped her a twenty.

She kissed the twenty and gave us a wave. "I'm gonna try."

I bounced Felicia up and down a little. "Are you getting down?"

"I'm debating. It's kind of nice up here. Warmer and I don't have to walk."

"I'm not carrying you around the Village." I had my limits. I let go of her legs.

She squawked and slid down off of me. "Spoilsport."

Even as I dropped her back down onto the sidewalk I realized something. Felicia made me laugh. She made me willing to do silly things. She made me step aside from my career for hours at a time and I couldn't even remember the last time that had been the case. My work was my life.

I'd been prepared to step back from my career to have a family, but now being around Felicia made it even easier than I'd been anticipating. I had thought it was going to be a true sacrifice, but now I had a totally different perspective.

It was a good realization.

I took her hand in mine. "A horrible spoilsport. Can we go home now since you're cold? Are we done with creating a deception that I doubt anyone will believe?"

"Absolutely. My joggers are calling my name. I ate too much. The ice cream put me over the edge of gluttony."

"Yet you ate a whole branzino the other night. I'm disappointed in you. Ice cream should be easy."

She laughed. "I think you should brag about that in our interview. What's something Felicia is great at?' 'She can eat a whole branzino in one sitting.'

"Oh, I'm totally going to mention that."

"If that's the top of the list of my talents, I need to reevaluate my life."

I squeezed her hand. "Nah. It's not even in the top ten of your talents."

Felicia glanced over at me. She smiled.

I realized in that moment, that simple, ordinary moment of

walking down the street holding hands, that I was already in love with her.

Well, fuck.

"ISN'T THIS COZY?" Felicia asked me as she snuggled up along-side me in bed.

It was, but I wasn't going to give it to her that easily. "You have a show about serial killers on. I don't think that qualifies as cozy."

The bedroom was warm though and despite her call for joggers on our walk, she had taken a hot shower and put on one of her silk nightgowns, so her bare leg was draped over mine. She'd made herself tea and her breath smelled like ginger. She'd said it was to settle her stomach.

It was all really damn domestic and yes, cozy.

"It's called compromise. That's what relationships are all about."

"How is that compromise?" I asked, wrapping my arm around her head and pulling her in closer on my chest. "You agreed to no murder shows in the bedroom and here we are watching some guy do some really bloody shit. And I see blood all the time at work, so if I'm disturbed, it's disturbing."

I'd preferred to read the book when it came to true crime. I didn't need the crime scene photos and reenactments.

"If it bothers you that much, feel free to change it," she said, though it sounded like she thought I was a massive wimp. "Though remember we're supposed to be showing each other our true selves."

"Thank you." I grabbed the remote and switched it to the basketball game.

"Basketball?" she said, sounding as disgusted as I felt over discussion of serial killer cannibalism.

"Yep." I kissed the top of her head. "This is my true self. Love it or leave it."

She stiffened against me. The words were far weightier than I had intended them to be. I was going to open my mouth and retract the words, or attempt to explain them away, when she propped herself up on my chest and stared intently at me.

"Michael?"

"Yes?" I waited, still, unable to read her expression.

"I'm feeling more inclined to love it than leave it these days," she murmured.

That made my gut tighten. "Glad to hear it," I said gruffly.

So maybe she was falling in love with me at the same time I was falling in love with her.

Felicia gave me a mysterious smile that did all kinds of things to my insides.

I picked up the remote. "Play ID TV," I said to it. The TV changed the channel back to her murder show.

She laughed and kissed me. "Thank you."

"Whatever."

That made her laugh even louder.

"SO HAVE you ever been married or engaged before?" Gloria asked me, spreading a thin layer of artisan butter over her focaccia bread.

It was a fair question and one that presumably would have come up more conversationally if Michael and I had been dating for a year. But it still caught me a little off guard.

"No, neither." Then because there was no reason to hide the truth, I said, "My last partner failed to mention he had a wife already. It was more than a bit awkward when she reached out to me. So I stepped away from dating for a while because it was very upsetting to have been made a cheat without my knowledge."

"Well, you weren't the cheat. Her husband was. You couldn't have known."

"No, I suppose not. There really weren't any red flags. But the time alone was good for me."

Gloria was scrutinizing me intently.

Why did I get the sudden feeling she was on to us?

"Seems like you would have some trust issues after an experience like that. Yet here you are engaged after just a few short months of dating."

I never should have told her about that bastard George. Because I did have trust issues. I struggled to take someone at face value and believe they really cared about me for me. But I was not going to divulge any of that to Gloria, clearly. "Hmm. You can't judge a man by another man's misdeeds."

"Good for you," she said, raising her wineglass. "Life is too short."

I waited for some further wisdom to follow but none seemed to be forthcoming. I just nodded and sipped my own wine. I wasn't sure what the hell was happening but I was definitely uncomfortable.

"Michael's been looking for a surrogate," she said. "But I'm sure you knew that already."

I choked on my wine. "Sorry?"

Now that was a hell of a bombshell to drop at lunch.

"He didn't tell you?"

She didn't really look surprised. If anything, she looked annoyed, which I couldn't interpret. I didn't know her well enough to get a read on her true emotions.

"He did not tell me, no." Not even a hint.

"He probably didn't want to scare you, but yes, that's how serious he's been about starting a family."

"I know it means a lot to him." I did know that. But damn. Michael had been willing to be a single father? Somehow that did surprise me. Then again, I'd never seen him around children.

Maybe it was time to babysit Savannah's baby. I felt like I needed to see Michael firsthand with a baby. Or maybe that would be a terrible idea. It might make me want to open the baby factory and it was way too soon for that. Like eighteen months too soon for that.

"I'd check the condoms for holes if I were you," Gloria said, with a tinkling laugh, like that was hilarious.

I had been distracted by my own thoughts but Gloria's casual and teasing statement was like a bucket of ice water over my head.

"What?" I slammed my wineglass down so hard it was a miracle it didn't shatter. Could I be pregnant already? I contemplated my uterus, questioning if I could feel an egg dividing in its depths. Nothing felt out of the ordinary. Didn't women just know instinctively?

"I'm kidding. Michael would never do something so dishonest."

Well, that was utterly reassuring. Not. I didn't think he would. Or at least I hoped he wouldn't. Because that would be very, very uncool.

"Why didn't he and Becca have children?" I asked, curious what her perspective on their marriage would be.

"Oh, she wasn't really interested, from what I understood at the time. She felt she was too young. I imagine that would have changed in a few years if she had lived. But it was a source of contention between them. Michael always felt like she overstated her desire for a family when they got engaged. A classic bait and switch."

Maybe I didn't need to worry so much about appeasing Becca's ghost. Having children or not was something you couldn't be dishonest about. That was just cruel to deny a man (or a woman) a child when they'd expressed such a strong desire for one.

"And then there was her spending. She never understood the meaning of the word budget. Plus there was the time I was certain she was having an affair with the contractor who redid their kitchen, but Michael would never confirm it. The contractor installed more than that island, if you catch my meaning."

Fabulous. Now I never wanted to lean on the island again. Or spread out my takeout over the surface without thinking of Michael's devious former wife.

Becca really was like Rebecca from the famed novel. Damn. I

didn't need to talk to her, I needed to sage her ass out of the closet. And order a new countertop for the island.

"I'm surprised Michael hasn't told you this himself. I probably shouldn't be telling you so many details about ancient history."

I loved when people expressed regret three seconds after sharing something juicy. As if they'd ever had any intention of not saying it. I was grateful for the insider information. "Oh, I think it's a tricky thing. Michael feels like if he talks about Becca too much I'll be worried he's not totally over her."

"That sounds like Michael. He's very considerate."

I couldn't really argue with that. "I'm honestly not worried about him being still hung up on her or anything like that. I don't get that sense from him at all and it's been ten years. Though I will be happy to buy a place we pick out together."

I was saying that as part of the overall grand plan, but the truth was, it did sound appealing. I could already picture what a new place together would look like. I was going to layer his minimal style with some dark moody velvets and plenty of texture.

There I was, making it real when it really wasn't.

Staying together was contingent on our feelings at the end of the month.

That thought was always in the back of my head. This might all just be for nothing in the end.

"Not to change the subject," Gloria said, "but we're limited on venues. Given it is December, availability is terrible and we're on a tight time frame. We can either move the party to the spring or settle for something less than ideal. I can't even get my event planner. She's totally booked out until February."

"Well," I said, because I didn't doubt she was right but I didn't like either option. I didn't want to commit to one over the other, so I drew the word out to buy some time. The wise thing to do would be to just proceed with a simple party, maybe even at Michael's flat, or Gloria and Bud's. Because the point really wasn't the party, it was what it represented—legitimacy for our engagement. It demonstrated our marriage displayed premeditation as opposed to an impulse for a visa.

Sort of like murder. Did it show intent or impulse?

Not that I was going to describe my engagement in murder terms. At least not to anyone but Michael. He might be amused by my thought process. Or not.

"Should we just have it at the flat?" I asked. It was a fake engagement party. I didn't need to book out The Plaza. "I'd rather not wait."

Gloria seemed as thrilled about the idea as I felt. "It is Michael's second marriage."

Now, hang on. I didn't think that was fair. Just because he'd been married before didn't mean I should get stiffed on quality.

Then I remembered it was fake anyway.

"We can just put the emphasis on catering," I said. "Everyone cares more about the food and the booze than the venue, right?"

"I wouldn't say that's entirely accurate but at least with it being the holidays we can go all out with the décor. Do you have a tree? I know Michael never has one and you just moved in."

"I have a tree. I fully decorated the flat. It was my first chance to go all out in years. My place was really small, so I went crazy at Michael's." Not to pat myself on the back or anything. "But we could use some rental tables and chairs or everyone will be standing the entire time." I pulled out my phone to make notes. "We should get the invites out tomorrow or the day after."

"I want paper. You can send electronic 'save the date ones' if you'd like, but thrown together or not, I want this to be a real engagement party," Gloria said.

Funny enough, so did I.

WHEN I GOT HOME I pulled dried sage out of my purse. I'd popped into a crystals and herb shop around the corner and gotten a bunch. I wasn't sure I believed in ghosts, but Becca felt ominous suddenly after my chat with Gloria. I didn't want to walk into the closet and find my entire wardrobe slashed in tatters.

I flicked on a lighter and ran it under the sage brush. It caught fire so I blew it out and let the smoke rise. I waved it around pretty frantically for maximum effect.

Okay, so maybe I did believe in ghosts. Or at the very least crazy wives hidden away that were supposed to be dead, like in the novel Jane Eyre. Oh my God, what if Becca wasn't dead?

"You're secretly a goth, aren't you?" Michael asked. "That's what you needed to reveal to me."

I jumped. "How do you do that? I never hear you come home! I could be burglarized before I even knew what hit me."

"How could you be robbed in our own apartment with a doorman and a key code entry?"

"I don't know. But criminals always find a way." I tried to nonchalantly put my hand on my hip as if the sage were an accessory. Only it was still burning, so a waft of smoke plumed up from my side. It rose into my nose and I resisted the urge to cough. I failed, but I kept my mouth clamped shut, so my cheeks ballooned out like a chipmunk. Finally, I gave in and burst out with a smoky cough.

Michael entered the closet and gave me a kiss. He looked deep into my eyes and said, "What the fuck are you doing?" in a very calm voice.

I turned to the left and breathed in some fresh air. "Saging the closet. It gets rid of old energy."

His eyebrows went up. "Jesus, we really need to move, don't we?"

"Sage is cheaper than moving."

"What brought this on?"

"Lunch with your mother."

That made him laugh. "That I can believe."

"And while I wouldn't call myself a goth, I do have a dark side."

"You have a dark side. I've gotten hints of that so far, but I'm going to need that described in a little more detail."

I didn't even consider myself having a dark side, but it was fun to tweak him a little. I did have nose rings and an entirely black wardrobe in high school but that was as far as I'd gone with it in terms of fashion choices. Watching crime TV and believing in ghosts didn't mean a thing. Those were just interests, not a lifestyle.

Time to change the subject. "What is this about a surrogate, by the way? Your mother mentioned you had been looking for one."

"Oh, geez, of course she did." Michael peeled off his suit jacket and threw it over his shoulder, holding it with one finger. "This is not a closet conversation. Can we sit down and eat something and talk?"

"Of course. We also need to talk about the fact that we never plan dinners. Maybe we need to sort that out too."

"I hate talking about dinner." He turned and went down the hall to the bedroom. "Can you figure out something for tonight? Please? I'll give you a thousand dollars."

That made me laugh as I poked my head out of the closet to watch him. "You're such a liar. You're not going to give me a thousand dollars. We have some of those premade salads in the refrigerator. Can you survive on one of those?"

"I'll hate every minute of it, but yes, I can survive on that."

He disappeared into the bedroom and I went back to my smudging. I moved the sage around in the closet before walking with the bundle down the hallway and into the kitchen. I liberally waved it over the island.

"You think the island is possessed?"

"No. I think there might be bad memories associated with the island."

Michael eyed me as he opened the cupboard and pulled a glass down. He was wearing workout clothes, so I expected he planned to go to the gym downstairs after we ate.

"How can a kitchen island hold bad memories? Unless it involves your cooking?"

"You're hilarious." I finished my wafting smoke around and put the sage in the sink. I pulled up some holiday music on my phone just to add some cheer. "Your mother might have mentioned that she thought there had been some infidelity on Becca's part, involving this specific kitchen island and its installation."

"Oh, God, my mother told you that? Wow." He filled his glass with water from the refrigerator door. "I'm not sure how that's any of her business or why she thought it would be okay to share something like that with you. She only knew about it because one night when Becca was sick and everyone was saying what a saint she was, I kind of lost my shit and implied it to my mother. Clearly a mistake."

"And don't forget Gloria told me that you were searching for a surrogate," I reminded him. "So I totally agree that she overstepped. Trust me, I wasn't fishing. I asked a few casual questions and she just spilled without hesitation. I'm not telling you to have you get upset with your mother, but I don't want to pretend not to know these things either. They're both kind of a big deal."

"No, I get it. I don't want you to feel awkward." He took a sip of water and set it down. On the island. "So one day I came home at lunchtime because I spilled queso on myself and I needed a clean dress shirt." He shrugged. "When I walked in, Becca was indeed getting fucked on the island by our contractor."

"Good God, that's just awful!" I felt horrible for him. "I'm so sorry."

"It was a long time ago. I can't say I forgave her, but I tried to. I do work a lot, especially back then. She felt neglected."

What an easy excuse. "If you feel neglected, you schedule a date night. You don't shag the contractor."

He nodded. "I agree. If she had told me how she was feeling, I could have at least tried to prevent it. But that's not the route she took. You can't stay angry with someone though when they get a raw deal like cancer at thirty years old."

I went into the refrigerator for the salads, realizing this was a good time for a confession of my own. It was embarrassing though and made me feel shameful even though I really hadn't done anything wrong. I stood up with the plastic containers in my hands. "I dated a man who was married and I had no clue he had a wife. I was gutted when I found out. Not only was I hurt and felt cheap and used, I felt absolutely awful for his wife."

It still made my stomach tighten when I gave it any real thought.

"Wow, that's a dirtbag move. What an asshole," Michael said. "What, like he couldn't find a woman who was willing to be his mistress? He had to lie about it?"

"It made me feel very disgusted, and frankly, disgusting. That's why I haven't dated. It was hard to trust anyone." It was hard to trust Michael, but I was trying. He didn't give me much reason not to trust him. He was very honest, as far as I could tell, and never hesitated to share when I asked him about his past. But then again, my ex had seemed honest as well. That was why our visa deadline scared me. I needed more time.

Anyone could pull off a con in six months or less. That's what ID TV and real life had taught me.

Michael pulled me into his arms. "I'm sorry he made you feel that way. What a selfish prick."

I let him hug me, because he smelled great and he had strong arms. Arms that made you feel protected. Cherished.

"We have a lot in common," Michael said. "More than you'd think at first glance."

"Well, we're both great in bed," I said, to lighten the mood.

He laughed. "Not what I had in mind. But very true." Michael pulled back and looked at me with naked lust. "Want to prove it?"

He had no idea how much I did. My insides ached for him.

But I'd said we had to abstain the whole time and I had to stick to it because what precedent would it set if he thought he could change my mind on anything?

"I'll pencil you in for January."

He groaned. "Fine. I'm going to skip the salad and hit the gym. I need to work out my sexual frustration."

"That's a very healthy approach, sweetheart, I applaud you, though you shouldn't skip meals." I gave him a sweet smile.

"You're really a witch, aren't you? It's the only explanation for why I agreed to celibacy."

That made me laugh. "I wish. I'd cast a spell on the person processing my application."

Michael went to the front closet and pulled out his running shoes. "It's worth a shot. We really need a yes from them."

I watched him, sitting down in the leather chair to put on his shoes. He sounded so casual, so matter-of-fact.

That he and I were a "we."

Given what that did to my heart, I had a strong suspicion that I'd already fallen halfway in love with Michael.

No amount of sage would dissipate that.

THIRTEEN

I RANG my mother while I was steaming clothes in preparation for a photo shoot.

"Hello, Felicia," she said.

"Hi, Mum, how are you?"

"Dreading Christmas with the cousins. Uncle Burton is such a lech."

"He is very quick with a perverted joke. Listen, what are you doing next weekend? Can you hop on a flight and come to New York?"

She laughed. "Not since your father left me practically destitute."

Destitute was an exaggeration but I ignored that. "My treat. I'm having a party and I'd like you here for it." I eyed a Chanel jacket for any pesky wrinkles remaining.

"What kind of party? You haven't joined a cult or something, have you?"

Where did she come up with these ideas? "No, of course not. Why on earth would I join a cult? I could never shave my head."

"It wouldn't be a good look on you," she said. "You had an egg head as a baby."

That made me laugh. "You keep me humble, Mum. It' not a

cult initiation. It's an engagement party. Michael asked me to marry him and I said yes."

I had never once mentioned Michael to my mother. But she barely paid attention to me on the best of days. Lately she'd been having a lot of bad days that she blamed on Hugh Grant. She said his aging made her feel appallingly old. Poor Hugh, it wasn't like the man had an agenda. Or could prevent the march of time.

She would never, ever admit she didn't know who Michael was.

"What? Well, congratulations, darling! How exciting. When did this happen? How did Michael pop the question?"

I bent over to trim a stray thread off the hem. "He took me to our favorite Italian restaurant and asked me first where I would like to live, if money were no object. I said the Upper West Side in a brownstone and he said then we'll start shopping."

My mother made a sound of approval. I knew she'd like that angle of the story.

"Then he pulled out a cushion cut Tiffany diamond and asked me to marry him."

"Well done, Michael."

That made me grin. "I thought so. I know it's a bit of a rush but I just have my heart set on a holiday engagement party." That had never once been something I'd craved, but we needed some explanation for the rush job that didn't cause people to conclude pregnancy or deportation.

"Will Michael's..."

I heard the pause while she fished for the right word that wouldn't reveal she had no idea who Michael was. I almost felt rotten for doing that to her, but my mother was notorious for humiliating me under the guise of concern on a fairly regular basis. We absolutely loved each other but that didn't mean we didn't have a touch of dysfunction. Or as she liked to call it, "fun with each other."

"Will Michael's parents be there?" I filled in, to help her out. I'm not totally heartless. "Yes, and his brother. I'm not sure if his sister can make it from California. But I need you here. Please." I did need her. I wanted to be able to hug my mother and have her somehow through the force of her cold British stare give me the strength to not fall in love with Michael.

Because so far, I was failing miserably. He was very easy to fall for. He was stubborn, confident, and used to getting his own way. But he was also generous, kind, and relatively easygoing. Not much seemed to irk him or put him in a bad mood and he laughed easily and frequently. None of my quirks even seemed to bother him.

It could be he was just on his best behavior, but I didn't think so. It all seemed very effortless, very true to who he really was as a man.

"I can't let you pay for my ticket. I'll sort it out, darling. Shoot me the details and I'll see what I can do."

"Thanks, Mummy. You're the best." I made kissing noises, which I knew she would hate.

"Gotta run, darling. I'll talk to you soon."

I tapped my screen to end the call after I said goodbye and eyed Becca's Chanel. I'd sold six pieces already but I would be happy when I'd seen the last of this lot.

My phone buzzed. It was a text from Michael with a link.

Something like this?

It was a real estate listing. The townhouse was beautiful. The perfect blend of original features with modern finishes. The first floor was an office and a family space that opened to the garden. I envisioned working there every day and felt warm.

"Ow, shit!" I realized I was actually burning myself with the steamer. My finger was red and angry.

Hopefully that wasn't a sign.

Somewhere Becca was laughing her cheating ass off.

"I CAN'T BELIEVE how much has changed in the last few months!" Savannah said, fully loaded after one martini.

We were out in Brooklyn again, and Savannah had just

finished weaning baby Sully off nursing. Her first sip of alcohol in something like fifteen months had gone straight to her head. She was gushing, leaning all over everyone, and saying repeatedly how much she loved her son, her boyfriend, Maddox, and us.

It was amusing, but I was already anticipating walking her home. I didn't trust her to get home safely on her own. I wasn't drinking because I had my engagement photo shoot the next night and I wasn't going to risk under-eye circles.

"I can't argue with that," Leah said. "I just had an engagement party a few weeks ago and I'm living with Grant, the man at the diner who hated on pancakes for six months. Who would have ever thought that would happen?"

"Not me," Dakota said, even though it was a rhetorical question. Dakota was wearing yet another outfit that fully demonstrated she embraced her height.

We'd had a break in the bad weather and so she was wearing heels that had to land her at six foot three. I had always admired her confidence.

"And of course, me," Savannah said. "Living with Mad, raising my son together." She gave a happy sigh. Then suddenly, like she'd just remembered, she pointed her finger at me, causing her drink to slosh over the rim. "And you! What the heck, Felicia? You were all, 'I don't date. And now you're engaged. You're fucking engaged. It's crazy."

She sounded almost outraged in her drunkenness, which made me laugh. "It's straight-up bonkers."

"That it is," Isla said under her breath, shaking her head and clearing her throat.

I was going to snark back at her, but Savannah reached across the table and smacked my hand.

"Why aren't you drinking?" Savannah demanded. "Get a drink, Felicia baby."

Felicia baby? She really was loaded. "I have my engagement photo shoot tomorrow. I can't be puffy and hungover."

"Ooh la la," Savannah said, rocking back and forth and doing some sort of jazz hands.

Dakota laughed. "What the hell is that?"

"What?" Savannah drained the last of her martini. "That was delish."

"Drink some water now," I told her. "You don't have your drinking legs anymore."

She threw her leg up in the air. "Yes, I do. Look at my leg."

We all laughed. Leah laughed so hard she choked.

"We're going to need to text Maddox and warn him what's coming home to him later," Isla said.

"His horny woman," Savannah said. "That's what's coming home to him. And finally, he can touch my boobs. This is going to be a good night."

More like a sloppy one but I didn't want to burst her bubble. I turned to Leah. "Have you set a wedding date yet?"

She shook her head. "No. I'm not worried about it. We have a vacation planned for Christmas. Fiji. How sexy is that?"

"Very," I agreed. "Is everyone here going to be able to make it to my engagement party? I will be crushed if you can't but I know it's super short notice."

"We'll be there," Savannah said. "I wouldn't miss it for anything. I need to find a sitter though."

"If you can't find a sitter, bring Sully. You know I love him." I did. The kid was a round-cheeked angel.

"Thanks, maybe I'll do that."

"Grant and I will be there too," Leah said. "I told him last night when we got your text."

"Of course I'll be there," Dakota said. "I am dying to meet Michael and I am also dying to see you with him. You're so reserved with dudes, I can't wait to see you all blushing and in love."

"Does she look like she's blushing?" Isla said. "I'm not buying this 'wildly in love' story, just saying."

"If you don't show up to this party, I will hunt you down and hurt you," I told her. "Plus, I'd never forgive you."

She rolled her eyes. "I'll be there. But only if you agree to drag out the engagement. You don't need to get married right now."

"You're blackmailing me for your presence? That's charming. You don't need to play the big sister role. I promise you I'm proceeding with caution. I adore Michael, but he does have flaws, and I have a bad track record."

The restaurant wasn't crowded at all and I was grateful I didn't have to shout. But it seemed to have slow service, which might explain a lack of diners. My water glass had been empty for five minutes and I couldn't seem to spot a server anywhere near us. Thinking about my past relationships made my throat dry.

"What are his flaws?" Dakota sounded gleeful. She sipped her cocktail and leaned forward to hear better.

She caught me off guard. "You want a list?"

"Yes," Isla said.

I frowned at our eternal cynic. "I didn't ask you, Isla.

"Michael doesn't have horrible flaws." He didn't. "It's mostly irritating things like leaving his beard hairs in the sink and his sterile taste in decorating. The fact that he punches his pillow repeatedly at night before he falls asleep. Wouldn't the first punch put it into the position you want?"

"I don't know," Savannah said. "Sometimes you really need to work it."

"Those are just pet peeves," Dakota said, waving her arm frantically to get the server's attention. "This service sucks. I'm going to order two drinks at once."

"Ooh, good idea," Savannah said.

I shook my head at her. "No. Not a good idea, Mommy. You're going to hate yourself tomorrow when you're hungover with a crying baby."

Her nose wrinkled, like she knew I was right and didn't want to accept it.

"What are the real flaws?" Isla asked. "The potential deal breakers?"

The fact that sometimes it felt like he withheld information. Like about his marriage and researching surrogates. But I wasn't sure if that was a character trait or just due to the speed of our relationship. There hadn't been time to just dump everything ever from our past onto each other. For that reason, I absolutely refused to reveal any niggle of doubt to my friends. If Isla weren't there, I might, but I wasn't even one hundred percent sure on that.

Time would tell. If it revealed Michael regularly lied by omission, I would tell my friends.

And not marry him.

Even though the thought of leaving him was getting harder and harder.

"He spends too much time focusing on me during sex," I said, dead pan. "I'm getting tired of all the orgasms." Which was true when we'd been having sex.

Isla shook her head.

Leah and Savannah laughed. Dakota looked puzzled for a second, then said, "Oh, ha ha, I get it."

"I thought you weren't having sex with him," Savannah said. "Which I think is such a shame."

"I'm not. Not since we moved in together." Though every night I questioned the logic in it. "I want to know how I feel about him, not his cock."

Though there no was denying I had quite the crush on both.

"DARLING, can you stop doing that with your mouth?" Felicia asked me.

"What, smiling?" I looked away from the photographer at my incredibly beautiful but picky-as-fuck fiancée. She'd been nonstop complaining since we'd started the stupid session twenty minutes earlier.

"That's not smiling. You're grimacing."

"I am not."

"Yes, you are. Why do you look so stiff?"

I raised my eyebrows in amusement. I was about to make a comment about my blue balls when she clapped her hand over my mouth.

"Don't say it."

"What?" I said, through her fingers. I pretended to bite one.

She pulled her hand back. "Beast."

"We're losing light," the photographer said. "Can we try that again?"

I actually wanted to walk into the nearest bar and order a bourbon. It was fucking freezing outside, again, but Felicia had insisted we do pictures in the park. I wasn't sure why it mattered but I wasn't going to argue with her.

"Of course," Felicia said. She squeezed my cheeks, trying to rearrange my mouth. "Can you just loosen up a little?"

"Baby, this is my face. I cannot change the way I look. It is what it is." Was my smile forced? Maybe. Because I felt stupid posing like I was twenty-five. The whole thing felt forced.

"Let's try something different," the photographer said, coming closer to us. The woman probably wanted the same glass of bourbon I did. "Just take a walk together, talk, do what you normally do when you're in the park. I'm going to follow you and see if I can get something more natural."

For a second I thought Felicia was going to protest but then I gave her my forced smile to demonstrate how much she thought I sucked at it and she relented. "It's worth a go. These clearly aren't working."

I took her hand and kissed the back of her knuckles. "Thank you. I'm a surgeon, not a model. That's your arena." That actually gave me an idea. "Hey, Agatha, would you mind taking a few shots of just Felicia? I think a few minutes watching her would really help me."

Felicia gave me a dirty look. "Why would there be pictures of just me for an engagement shoot? I'm not marrying myself."

"Just indulge me." I wanted to see her do her thing. Or her former thing, anyway. "You can pose so the ring is visible."

"Whatever you want to do is fine with me," Agatha said.

She sounded bored. She was also like twelve. She reeked of youthful arrogance. I wondered if I had been like that in my twenties. Probably.

"Fine. Point out where you want me to stand, Agatha," Felicia said.

They had a few minutes' discussion, heads huddled. Then Felicia moved in front of a large rock and pushed her hair back and tilted her head toward the wind so her hair would move behind her. She took one hand and gripped the opposite wrist as she slightly turned her body. Her lips parted and she gave a sultry mysterious stare. It stunned me how easy it was for her. I'd seen some of her runway shots and of course, for her clothing sales, but seeing her outside, just shifting and turning easily, naturally, it made me aware of how absolutely gorgeous she was and in tune with her own body.

She raised her hand and pulled her hair, pulling it over her chin, in a move to display the ring but that was also super sensual.

I realized there was so damn much I still didn't know about Felicia. We were at the beginning, and while we were rushing it with the engagement, I didn't want to rush it any further than that. We could get married when the fiancée visa was going to expire but maybe I didn't need to push her to have a baby right away. Maybe it would be smart to just spend some time together, as a couple. Who cared if I was a year older when a family happened? I wanted the pleasure of learning everything I could about my fiancée.

Felicia climbed onto the rock. In heels. Damn. She perched on it in a way that was fierce and sexy. She was wearing a sweater and jeans but still, the three-inch boots should have made her pose impossible. Everything about it was so fucking hot that I decided I could join her. I walked over and found a foot hold in the rock and climbed up beside her.

She gave me a very naughty and pleased look.

I cupped her cheek and kissed her.

She kissed me back, passionately.

The rock was cold and uncomfortable, but I pulled back and stared into her blue eyes. My hand slipped down over her hip. I could never get close enough to her. "You are the sexiest woman I've ever met."

She gave me a smile. "Flattery will get you everywhere. In January."

"Is it January yet?"

"No. But it's only fifteen days away."

"I'm going to make you scream my name, sweetheart. And I can't wait."

Her lips parted on a small gasp.

"I think I've got some good stuff," Agatha called. "Though this may be the first engagement shoot where I feel like I could get pregnant from watching. Phew. Hot stuff."

That broke the mood. Felicia laughed.

I helped her down off the rock and took her hand and kissed it. "Maybe we can find somewhere between me being super awkward and us eye fucking each other. Otherwise we're going to have some explaining to do to friends and family."

"I'm certainly up for that. We can find an in-between, I believe in us."

"As soon as we're done here I want a bourbon. A big one."

"I want a big one too but we can't always get what we want." She bit her bottom lip and raised her eyebrows up and down.

That made me groan. She was just evil. Amazing. Intelligent. Sexy as hell.

And I would do anything to make sure she stayed in New York as my fiancée.

FOURTEEN

HAVING SPENT the better part of a year at home working behind a camera or behind my computer screen I was worried my social skills would be rusty. But I found I was actually really enjoying interacting with Michael's colleagues and of course, the children who were the special guests for the orthopedic department's Christmas party fundraiser.

Michael had told me that he had debated pediatric orthopedics back in med school but hadn't felt like he could stay emotionally removed enough. He'd felt much more comfortable working with adults.

But watching him interact with the kids proved that he might not be the right surgeon for a child, but he was an awesome advocate and friend. He was full of high fives, dad jokes, and hugs. After being introduced to a flurry of people I had hung back while he greeted the kids and their parents. He'd told me most had suffered some sort of traumatic bone injury due to a car crash or things of that nature. A few had been born with genetic malformations and watching their joy at this event had me tearing up.

It was a fundraiser, but it was also a Christmas carnival, complete with an indoor Ferris wheel and Santa's workshop at the

North Pole. I was surprised Michael hadn't campaigned to be Santa Claus himself but he said the hospital hired an actual actor every year. When he'd first told me one of his demands was that I attend his work holiday party with him, I'd been picturing a traditional cocktail party with little black dresses, an open bar, and awkward small talk with people juggling tapas plates in their hands.

This was a thousand times better than that. I felt like I'd fallen into holiday happiness. The music was cheerful, the decoration larger-than-life, with a toy theme, and I was sipping a non-alcoholic egg nog. Given it was only two in the afternoon, I had been happy to have the virgin alternative. I also had to admit I had stationed myself so I could readily cruise past all the food options, of which there were many. I was starving and I had no idea why but everything I put in my mouth tasted fabulous, so I just kept grazing.

"These mini crème brulees are amazing, aren't they?"

I turned and saw Kim, who Michael had introduced as his surgical assistant. I smiled at her. "It's shocking how much I've eaten. I should be mortified but I can't bring myself to care."

"It's still a week until Christmas," she said. "By New Year's I'm going to need new clothes." She didn't look like she cared one iota either though as she loaded a plate up with pastries.

"Do you have any fun New Year's Eve plans?" I asked, to try to be conversational. Michael spoke about Kim in a way it was clear he valued her as a co-worker and as a person.

She nodded, giving me a smile. "This year my girlfriends and I are going to Miami Beach. I can't wait to get out of here for a week."

"That does sound fun. I've never been to Miami Beach. I have been to Ibiza though, which is a very sexy place." I picked up another plate. Why the hell not?

"Do you and Dr. K have plans?"

Nothing I could say out loud. Given what Michael had said during our engagement photo shoot his plan was to keep me in bed all day giving me orgasms. I certainly wasn't going to object to that.

Assuming that we both agreed to stay together and ride out the visa process.

God, I'd be gutted if he didn't want to do that.

I shook my head. "We haven't discussed it yet. We've been focused on our engagement party. In four days. Yikes." The end of the year and the end of my visa were coming up fast. I tried to ignore the anxiety that thought brought up.

"Congratulations, by the way. I'll be there at the party, but I'm sure you know that."

"I appreciate you coming. I realize everyone is jam-packed with events this time of year." I was wearing extremely tight black jeans and wishing I could undo the top button on them because they were digging into my flesh. It was either overindulging or a tightening from anxiety about the possibility of Michael changing his mind. I debated if my sweater would camouflage it if I did let it free. I popped a sweet potato puff wrapped in bacon into my mouth.

"Dr. K is a really nice guy, you know," she said.

I paused mid-chew and nodded. "I realize that."

"No. I mean he's one of the best. I hope you appreciate that."

Ah, so a little warning. I liked that Michael inspired loyalty in his friends.

I looked over at where Michael was lifting a little boy up into the air and whirling him around.

Everything inside of me swelled up at the sight of him. Kim was right. He was a really nice guy. One of the best.

"I do appreciate it," I said, and I could hear the softness and affection in my own voice. "I appreciate him."

Kim must have heard it too because she gave me a smile. "Glad to hear it. By the way, don't get the wrong impression. I don't have a crush on him or anything. We're just friends."

I laughed. "That never crossed my mind, but I'd forgive you if you did. I've been desperately trying to find flaws in him and failing miserably."

"He's stubborn, if that helps," Kim said, with a grin.

"Oh, trust me, I do know that." Yet, he wasn't unwilling to compromise.

He was the total package and I had utterly betrayed myself and all of my intentions by going and falling completely and totally in love with him.

Massive idiot, that was me.

As usual.

What the hell would I do if none of this worked out? If we didn't work out?

Suddenly, without warning, I felt tears in my eyes.

Oh, fuck, how awkward was that?

Michael was coming over to us, carrying a toddler in his arms, presumably the child's mother walking beside him.

I dabbed my eyes with my napkin desperately, but Kim had already seen the tears. She shot me a look of alarm.

Michael's eyes widened and his smile fell off his face. "Are you okay, Felicia?"

I nodded, sniffing. "Just too much hot sauce," I lied. "I'm fine."

Obviously, Kim would know I was lying since I hadn't eaten anything with hot sauce, but I couldn't worry about it.

The introductions were a blur but I put on a smile and was polite. It turned out the mother was a colleague of Michael's, a fellow surgeon. I looked at her toddler, a little girl who had deep brown eyes. She wasn't smiling. She was staring at me with such intensity, I could have sworn she was on to me. It was like she knew Michael and I were lying to everyone and the government and playing a very dangerous game.

That made me mentally shake my head. She was a toddler. She was probably just staring at my red lipstick or my necklace and I was fucking losing it.

So maybe the kid didn't know anything but when I turned, looking for somewhere I could get a glass of water, I saw Kim watching me.

It was not a nice look. It was a hate-filled expression of pure rage.

She had lied about not having a crush. Our gazes met and she rapidly looked away.

I didn't even care. Let her crush on him all she wanted. If the man had even once ounce of interest in her he'd have made a move in the years they'd worked together.

The only concern it gave me was if she chose to be a bitch and tell INS we were stretching the truth about the length or depth of our relationship. If she did, then she was just a miserable cow.

I felt nauseous and I wanted a glass of water. "I'm sorry," I said, rudely interrupting the conversation going on around me. "I desperately need some water, so excuse me a minute. I'll be right back."

Michael was handing the toddler back to her mother and looking concerned. "I can go get some for you."

"No, no, it's fine." I couldn't stand there and guarantee I wasn't going to tear up again, which was absurd. "I'll be right back."

I turned and blindly set my plate down on a high-top table.

"She was really pale," the woman said, whose name I honestly couldn't remember even though I'd been told it five minutes earlier. "She's either coming down with something or she's pregnant. I recognize that expression of trying not to lose your lunch."

"Maybe she's hungover," Kim offered.

I didn't even pause to debate why the hell Kim would suggest something like that as I rushed off, terrified by Dr. Whoever's statement.

Pregnant?

No. I couldn't be.

That would be so not cool.

Forgetting all about water, I fast walked in the direction of the restrooms.

I made it to the ladies' room, but not to a stall. I spotted a trash can right at the entrance, twisted my hair back, and tossed all the heavy appetizers into it.

God. I retched until there was nothing left in my stomach.

I stood up, vision blurred from watering eyes. I wiped them

with the back of my hand and reached for the towel dispenser with shaking hands. I blotted my eyes and my forehead and went to wash my hands.

Michael's doctor co-worker was right. I looked pale and sallow. It had to be stress and anxiety.

Anything else was too much to think about.

THE STRESS WAS STARTING to get to Felicia. That was obvious. She was pale and not eating well. After my co-worker Shelia had suggested maybe she was pregnant, I had debated that, but dismissed it. We had only had two nights together, and we'd been very cautious. Those nights hadn't even been that long ago. It seemed a few weeks too early for real morning sickness.

She wasn't sleeping well and I thought that was contributing to why she looked so pale and drawn. And the reason she wasn't sleeping well was clearly our current situation.

Quizzing each other on facts about ourselves so we could pass an immigration interview wasn't exactly relaxing. Plus, my mother had been blowing up her phone about the damn engagement party and Felicia's own mother had decided not to fly to New York for it, which had greatly upset her.

We were drinking coffee the day before the engagement party. We had a full day ahead of us. An appointment with the lawyer, and then we were going to look at three apartments for sale. After that, most likely I would lose her to the final details of the party, which had truthfully become something I was dreading. The whole thing had been a lot of work for her. As Felicia shifted papers around in front of her on the coffee table, her hair the very definition of bedhead, I regretted we hadn't skipped the party.

"The tables and chairs will be delivered tomorrow at noon," she said, reaching for her mug. She wasn't looking where she was reaching, and she bumped it, spilling coffee over the rim. "Bloody hell."

"Sweetheart, what do you need me to do?" I asked, using the sleeve of my ribbed shirt to mop up her coffee. It wasn't that much and she was on the edge. "I feel bad this has all fallen on you."

She blotted her papers with her napkin. "It's my mess. Literally. I'm the one without the proper visa. So it *should* fall on me."

"I meant more the party, but still, you don't need to be dealing with any of it alone. That's what I'm here for. We're partners." I meant that. I loved Felicia. With all of my heart. It might be crazy to fall for someone that soon after knowing them, but we'd been in a crash course on compatibility and she was *it* for me. The one.

Not that I'd told her. I was waiting for the moment when we had to make the decision on whether she was staying in New York, with me, or letting her visa expire and returning to England. That had been her plan all along. No sex. Follow the rules. Then we would each make a decision how we felt at the end of the forty days.

I knew my decision and I knew how I felt.

I wanted her. Forever.

She looked less certain about the whole thing. I still needed to plead my case.

Felicia finally sighed and looked up. "I know and I appreciate you for offering. You're really a sweetheart. I'm just run a bit ragged and my mum not coming to the party is upsetting me. She's being stubborn about letting me pay for a plane ticket."

"I guess that's where you get your stubbornness, then."

She laughed lightly. "I guess so." She tugged the sides of her satin robe tighter around her. "I swear to God, Michael, I've gained weight. Even this bloody robe feels tight."

Again, I thought that was anxiety manifesting itself physically. "You don't look one ounce heavier. I think you're just stressed and not sleeping well and everything feels off. You were up half the night tossing and turning last night."

She made a face. "Did I wake you?"

"No. My sexual frustration is keeping me up at night, but since

I was awake too, yes, I noticed." I was only half-kidding about that. It was hell to lie in bed next to her, feel her bodily warmth, press my lips to hers, and have to stop. It was a crime against my manhood.

"Subtle." She picked up her coffee mug and sipped. "This is cold and I swear our creamer has gone off." She made a face and set it down. "I can't drink that."

This was going to be an awesome day. Not. But I was determined to keep calm and be supportive for Felicia. My coffee tasted fine to me, but I said, "Why don't you go get ready and I'll go around the corner and get some coffee?"

She nodded. "I think a hot shower would help."

Even more reason for me to be out of the apartment. I didn't need the temptation of her naked and wet in the shower.

"Perfect. Then we can head to the lawyer's office."

An hour later we were midtown sitting in front of the lawyer again. He was going over our prenuptial agreement in extreme detail, making sure everything was listed correctly in the documents he'd had printed up.

"If everything looks okay to you, then I just need your signature here," he said, pointing to the spot where a sticky note had been place with an arrow. "And everywhere you see an arrow."

"It looks fine to me." It was a basic document allowing us both to exit the marriage with what we'd entered with, including my car and apartment. I signed everywhere that was required, wondering why we couldn't have done this electronically, but figuring we could use the opportunity to check on her application process.

"Do you have any questions, Felicia?" the lawyer asked. "Technically I work for Michael, but I can answer anything you'd like clarification on."

That was a very lawyerly thing to say. I wondered if it would piss Felicia off, but she'd told me she had a headache, even after she'd had a latte. She looked like she was wishing she had a soft bed to sleep in for about a week.

"It all sounds aboveboard to me," she said. "Where do I sign?"

Once that was out of the way, I asked, "Any news on Felicia's visa application?"

He shook his head. "No. But I wouldn't expect anything this soon. What we need to discuss is your options at this point. You're down to two weeks before the expiration. The smartest and most appropriate course of action is for Felicia to return to the UK temporarily prior to the expiration while waiting for approval on the fiancée visa. It shows that she respects the laws of the immigration process. The downside though, is once she's out of the US they might not let her back in."

I'd known, theoretically, that they wouldn't process our visa request before the expiration but I hadn't been thinking she would have to return to England anyway. "That sounds risky."

"All your options are risky. If she stays, it might be held against her, and then her visa denied. Your other option is to get married, skip the fiancée visa, and apply for a spousal visa. You can plead ignorance, that it was always your intention to get married at Christmas, and you didn't really think it would be an issue. Usually they don't hold it too much against you if you get married as long as you can prove your relationship is legitimate. The other option would be to go to the UK together, get married there, and wait for the spousal visa to be approved. Or get married here and go to the UK to wait."

Holy shit. My head was spinning. "That's a lot of options."

He nodded. "Some riskier than others. My recommendation is to get married here in the US, prior to the visa expiration, then Felicia returns to the UK to wait out the approval process. Legally, that is the option that violates no rules or regulations."

I just sat there, taking that in.

Felicia cleared her throat. "How long does a spousal visa take?"

"It just depends. Usually with the UK they're pretty quick. Three to six months."

Six months wasn't the end of the world. "What if they don't approve the visa at that point?"

"You can apply again. Or move to the UK."

"I'm a surgeon," I said. "I can't exactly move my career to England."

"I understand. I'm just telling you the facts."

The facts kind of sucked.

Felicia sighed. "Well. Thank you for all the information. We'll let you know if we need the visa application changed to spousal or if we just want to cancel it."

I frowned at her. "We're not canceling it. We just need to go over our options." I stood up and held my hand out to the lawyer. "Thanks for all your help, we appreciate it."

Felicia stood up and did the same.

We left and neither of us said a single word down the hallway, in the elevator, or as we walked across the lobby of the office building. I was kind of waiting for her to speak first, curious where her head was. Did her comment about canceling it mean she didn't want to be with me? As in, I was in love with her and she was absolutely not in love with me?

The minute we got out on the sidewalk, she rammed her purse strap further up on her shoulder, adjusted her hat and said, "This is just bullshit. Those are our options? We can either be dodgy as hell and hope for the best or I have to go back to England anyway? If that's the case, what was the fucking point of any of this?"

Her cheeks were red, her eyes blazing.

I could see a lot of points to this but I wasn't going to debate that with her. "You wouldn't be going back permanently. Just until the visa is approved."

"So we rush a wedding, get married in a courthouse months before we reasonably should, and then I have to leave so we can't even continue to develop our relationship? That is just insane."

She had a very valid point. "I agree it is not ideal. Do you want to go get some lunch while we discuss this? I'm starving." Unlike her, I actually had an appetite.

My attitude was we came out bold and brazen. Get married, stay in the US. Act like we'd been planning a wedding the whole damn time. Turn the engagement party into a surprise wedding. I thought she needed to be sitting down though before she heard my idea.

Maybe I was just used to getting what I wanted, but I felt confident we would be victorious in the end of this whole process.

FIFTEEN

THE MAN WANTED LUNCH. My whole life was crumbling around me and he needed a bloody sandwich?

"By all means, let's get lunch," I said and my voice sounded high-pitched and a bit insane. I felt insane.

It was all my own fault. I'd brought all of this on myself. I'd been careless and stupid and should have somehow worked all this out years ago. I should have hired a man on the dark web to be my husband. I could have been married and divorced and happily a permanent resident by now.

Michael suggested a restaurant across the street, and because I cared not one damn bit where he ate, I nodded. My stomach was in knots. I couldn't eat if my life depended on it. I just wanted a glass of water. Fortunately, it was the kind of restaurant where there was enough of a hum no one else could overhear your conversation, but not so loud you had to shout.

"I guess I'm going back to London," I said, after we ordered drinks. "I can sleep on Mum's couch for a while. We'll just wait for the fiancée visa."

"That's not our only option," Michael said.

"It's technically the only legal one."

"The lawyer didn't say it was illegal, did he? I don't remember that specifically." Michael scoured the menu. "The cowboy chili sounds good."

The thought of beans and their texture made me want to throw up in my mouth, so I just stayed silent on his lunch ponderings. "We can't get married before the expiration date. That's just irresponsible."

"And here I was thinking that we should go for it. We can tell all our friends and family the engagement party is actually a wedding. That's a trend now, you know. Surprise weddings."

"How the fucking hell do you know what is trending with weddings?" I demanded. "That's absurd." God, my stomach hurt. I rubbed it as discreetly as possible. I didn't mean to have such attitude but I was stressed to the max. "I'm sorry. I'm not trying to be a bitch."

"Look what you could manage if you were trying," he said with a grin.

Despite my anxiety, that did actually make me smile. "You should live in fear of that. But seriously, Michael, we can't do that. It's just too much pressure. It's like driving off a cliff. We're already living together and applying for this fiancée visa. I don't think we should impulsively get married on top of it all."

"Let's just think about it before we make any final decisions."

"Our engagement party is tomorrow!" I felt my throat tighten. The room momentarily went black and I saw stars. "Oh, Jesus," I whispered, afraid to move my head.

"Are you okay?"

The blackness receded. I took some frantic breaths. "I thought I was going to pass out for a second. Everything went black."

"Maybe we should skip seeing the apartments today. Maybe you should try to take a nap."

For some reason, that made me angry. "I don't want to take a nap. I want to see the damn apartments."

His mouth opened. His mouth closed. Finally, he said, "Sure. Great."

It was an indication of his maturity that he just let me act like a psychopath and didn't react in anger. I was instantly mollified. "I should order some soup. Maybe it will settle my stomach."

"Great idea. Maybe something clear, like a vegetable soup with a broth base."

For a minute, we just sat there, him looking like he was debating calling the bomb squad to defuse me, me trying to process how and why I was utterly losing my shit.

Too much change in a short amount of time.

During which I had fallen in love.

I hadn't been planning on falling in love.

That was the exact opposite of the plan.

But I was starting to think I'd already been halfway in love with him, then had fallen the rest of the way when I met him in person.

Love at first sight. In a way.

It certainly had shook my world upside down.

I hadn't even told Michael I was in love with him. I didn't want it to influence his decisions about how to proceed from there, but it was hard to look at him and stuff down my emotions. Now I really felt like I had to keep quiet. He was suggesting we get married.

The. Next. Day.

My stomach lurched again.

Did that mean he loved me? Or was he just assuming eventually he'd love me? Or that we'd have a baby and love would be a friendly thing, based on sexual chemistry and co-parenting.

It felt like the words were stuck inside me, scratching at my throat and mouth, trying to burst forth with a scream.

I love you.

I wanted him to say it first. I needed him to say it first.

Maybe that was why I felt so fucking nauseous. I was choking on my own emotions.

When the server appeared to disrupt our loud and painful silence, I cleared my throat and managed to ask her for a cup of minestrone soup.

Michael settled on a bacon burger. With fries. A side of the chili.

Good God. I was grateful the table was wider than a standard two-top. I didn't want to be close enough to smell any of that.

"We couldn't even get a marriage license by tomorrow," I said, as the thought popped into my head. Not that I was considering marrying him, but it truly wasn't even possible.

"We could go get one today if we really wanted to."

"I don't think so," I said, even though I was basing that on nothing. "I think there's a waiting period."

"I can look it up online and find out." He pulled out his phone.

I shook my mind. "Don't do that. We can't get married tomorrow. That's just... overwhelming. Especially with fifty people in the room, watching us. I just couldn't."

"We could get married at the courthouse, then have the engagement party be an actual wedding reception. We can surprise everyone."

"I don't know." I didn't. I didn't know anything. I sipped my water and watched Michael swipe through his phone, clearly looking up marriage licenses.

If he had said he wanted to marry me tomorrow because he loved me, with all his heart, and wanted to be together forever and build our relationship into something amazing, I might be stupid enough to agree to it. But he wasn't saying he loved me. He was saying it was the practical thing to do and I didn't think I could stand there and have it be fake when I wanted it to be real.

Even if he said he thought he was falling in love with me, that it could be the foundation for something more, I might have been tempted.

What he was suggesting wasn't even close.

"This is actually a pretty simple process. You go in person to the courthouse and fill out the application. It's processed while you wait, then you have to wait twenty-four hours before you can get married. So we could go back tomorrow and get married or find someone to marry us at the party."

I didn't even know what to say.

"All I need is Becca's death certificate. You've never been married, have you?" he asked.

That right there made it ridiculous. How could we get married when he didn't even know if I'd been married before?

"I have not been married before, no."

Something about my tone must have alerted him that I was on the edge of hysteria. He finally glanced up from the screen. "Are you okay?"

I shook my head. "Not really. You're discussing getting a marriage license like we're picking up a pizza. Get it while you wait."

"I don't want you to leave the country," he said. "My concern is you won't be allowed reentry."

Again, so romantic. I was happy to hear that he didn't like the idea of me being gone permanently, but it still wasn't exactly a love declaration. "I'm concerned about that too."

"I can't live in England. It's not even a maybe until I'm retirement age. Which contrary to what some people think is not anytime soon."

"I know that." The waitress appeared with our lunches and I actually thought my soup looked appetizing. When she left, I took a small spoonful. It almost immediately settled my stomach, thank goodness. "Can we just maybe let it all sit for a minute and talk about this later today? It feels very manic to make an instant decision."

Michael had a mouthful of burger and couldn't respond. He was the oddest eater, vacillating between barely eating at all and smashing on huge meals. I guess it wasn't odd to him, but to me it felt unpredictable. I would have preferred he be in a healthy mood today but obviously not.

I sipped my soup and waited.

But he didn't react to my statement at all. He just changed the subject. He asked me how the sale of Becca's clothes was going.

The abrupt shift surprised me but I was relieved. I didn't want to argue about the visa.

"Actually, it's almost completely sold out. There are only a few stragglers still up for sale on the site. I'll have a fair amount of money to transfer to you next week."

He nodded. "Great. I'll donate it then."

"I think that's very generous of you." It was. I wanted to say more, ask more, but instead I just sipped my soup.

He bit his burger and didn't elaborate.

Our vibe was off. The lunch felt weird, the day felt strained. What the hell was going on?

He must have felt it too because this time when he changed the subject it had nothing to do with us personally. He asked me, "What's the strangest thing you've ever seen on one of your murder shows?"

I appreciated the effort to stay away from hot topics, so I just shrugged. "Oh, geez, there are so many things people have done that are bonkers. I think the ones that are literally so stupid in their planning aren't as interesting as the devious ones. Who murders three family members with antifreeze over eighteen months and thinks no one will be on to you?"

"Someone who really hates their family, I guess."

"People are nuts." I gave him a smile. "Thank you for trying to distract me. I appreciate the effort."

"I'd really like to distract you by getting you naked and driving you crazy, but that's against the rules, so I'm stuck with crime TV."

That made me laugh. He looked forlorn.

"Maybe we can work something out. Bend the rules a little." If I had to go back to the UK before my visa expired, I was not stepping foot on a plane without having sex with Michael first. That didn't give us much time.

"Don't tease me. Is that an actual offer?"

"Not today, because I feel like hell from not sleeping, so don't try to run me home for a quickie before apartment hunting. But yes, it's an actual offer." He wasn't the only one being tormented by nights lying in bed next to each other. Not only did I want him physically, I wanted the intimacy it brought.

"That turned my day around completely," he said. "I am really fucking happy now."

Sure, because he wasn't the one who felt like they had a golf ball in their throat.

I love you.

I swallowed the words. Again.

I COULDN'T READ Felicia as we toured the second apartment. The first she hadn't liked at all. It was too narrow, with very little natural light. I hadn't bothered to point out that was the nature of a brownstone. With this one, she was very quiet. She wasn't verbalizing any dislikes. But she wasn't saying she liked it either.

Her mood had been off all day and I hated to see her so stressed.

To me the logical thing to do was to get married but I wasn't going to push it. She'd made it pretty damn clear that was not something she wanted to do. Not today, anyway. Or even tomorrow.

The real estate agent was pointing out how high tech the apartment was.

Which was great, but not the most important thing. You could update or upgrade anything, but you couldn't change location, which with this brownstone was amazing. You couldn't change the overall footprint either and I had no complaints on the bones of this townhouse.

To me, this place was a slam dunk. The outdoor space was beautiful and private, with very little upkeep required. Getting a garden in Manhattan was a major score. The doors to the backyard were accordion style, so when the weather was nice, you basically eliminated the wall to the outdoors. I could see entertaining in this place, with its huge kitchen and massive island. I could see having kids here, running up and down between the kitchen and family room level and the garden level.

I saw all of those things with Felicia.

But I couldn't tell you what she saw, if anything. I felt like in a month I'd gotten to know Felicia as deeply as if we'd spent a year together. Then there were times she remained a mystery. She claimed it was because she was British and trained by her mother to keep her feelings private. I had no idea if that was true or not, but I did find it frustrating sometimes. Now was one of them.

I felt like the real estate agent agreed with me. She was a woman named Krisha, in her fifties, very polished, looking for any sort of clue as to what Felicia was thinking.

"Who is the cook in the relationship?" she asked with a smile.

"We don't really have one," I said. "Though I can make something work as needed."

"I can't stand to cook," Felicia said. "So much work."

The agent laughed. "No wonder you're so thin, then."

"It is a gorgeous kitchen," Felicia said, running her hand across the quartz countertop. "It's really perfect for entertaining, isn't it?"

I wasn't sure who was more excited, me or the agent, to have her positive reaction.

"Top-of-the-line appliances, which even if you don't cook, are perfect for having a personal chef or caterers in. It's so rare with a brownstone to have the width for such a deep island. This one is truly an anomaly."

"I really like the outdoor space," I said. "What do you think, sweetheart?"

She nodded and smiled. "It's all very nice. Can we see the bedrooms?"

"Absolutely." The agent ushered us toward the stairs. "Is this your first home together?"

I waited to see if Felicia would answer and she did. "We live together now but it's a flat Michael shared with his first wife. I want something we picked out together."

FORTY DAY FIANCÉ   173

Did Becca really bother her that much? I wasn't even really sure.

"So understandable," the agent said. "Memories are like cobwebs. You think you've got them all cleared out and then you find some lingering."

"Exactly. Is there a powder room?" Felicia asked, suddenly sounding brisk. She set her purse down on the island. Or more accurately, threw it.

"There is one right by the front entry, next to the study. So convenient to have a bathroom on every floor."

Except Felicia wasn't asking as a buyer. She jogged across the house, a desperate look on her face. She didn't even have a chance to close the door behind her before we heard her throwing up.

"Oh, dear." The agent looked sympathetic. "Morning sickness?"

I shook my head. "No, she's not pregnant."

She looked like she had a differing opinion on that. "You might want to look into it to be sure. I hope it's not the flu."

I chewed on that as I went to check on Felicia. She was hovering over the toilet, pale, breathing deeply. "Hey." I smoothed her hair back off of her face. I wasn't stupid enough to ask if she was okay, when she clearly was not. "Do you need some water or a cold cloth or something?"

"A cloth would be fantastic."

Fortunately, the brownstone was not occupied. It had been remodeled by an investor, so there was actually a box of disposable hand towels on the vanity. I pulled one out and wetted it under the faucet. I lifted the back of her hair and pressed it against her neck. Then I flipped it over and did the same to her forehead.

"Should I grab us a cab or do you need to wait a few minutes? I can go see the upstairs with Krisha if you want to just sit."

"Just give me a second. I want to see the bedrooms. I really like this place." She looked up at me. "But does it make sense to invest in real estate if I'm being tossed out of the country?"

"Even if you have to go to the UK, it won't be forever. Just a few months. If you really like this place, we should make an offer. This is a great street, it's super quiet."

Felicia wiped her mouth. She tossed the towel in the toilet and flushed. "Help me up."

I offered her a hand. Once she was standing, she actually hooked her arm through mine and leaned on me.

What if she was pregnant? That would be both amazing and terrifying. I hadn't pictured having a baby this soon. Talk about jumping in with both feet, damn.

She didn't comment on it at all or offer any explanation for her sudden nausea, so I kept my mouth shut too even as my heart rate kicked up a notch or twelve.

The third floor had three bedrooms, a laundry room, and a bathroom clearly designed for children. It had a trough-style sink and a ton of built-in storage. The fourth floor was a massive master suite with a spa bathroom. Krisha chattered away and I picked up the slack for Felicia's silence, talking finishes and square footage.

When we got back downstairs Felicia retrieved her purse from the island and hugged it to her stomach. "I think we should skip seeing that last listing today," she said. "I want to lie down."

"Of course, take care of yourself. Let me know if there's anything else I can do for you."

"I'll be in touch," I told Krisha. "Thank you for meeting us today."

When we got outside I didn't have a chance to ask Felicia anything.

She just put her hat on as we went down the steps and looked at me. "Michael?"

"Yes?" Why did that sound so fucking ominous?

"If we don't get this house, I might actually die."

That made me laugh, out of both relief and the dramatics of it. "So you like it?"

"I fucking love it. I will battle demons from hell if it means I can live in this house. It's everything."

"Maybe I should call Krisha right now." I stood on the sidewalk and looked up at the house. It was a family home. If Felicia wanted to move here, she must want permanency with me. Then again, she didn't want a marriage license, so I had no fucking clue what she truly wanted.

"Maybe we should think about it." She looked up at the house with me, leaning against my arm.

I pulled her in to my chest and gave her a little squeeze. "Thinking is overrated. I've been doing it my whole life and what did it get me? Sometimes you just have to feel something."

"Then I feel like I'm home," she murmured.

I kissed the top of her fuzzy hat. "Me too."

Pulling my phone out, I told it, "Call Krisha."

SIXTEEN

THE DAY WAS PURE CHAOS.

There were strangers all over our flat setting up tables and chairs and prepping for the catering. There was hustling and bustling and chopping and chatter.

I wanted to throw up again.

Savannah came through the front door and hugged me. "Honey, it's going to be okay."

"I don't know that it is, Savannah. If this test is positive, what the hell am I supposed to do?" Michael was out buying alcohol for the party and his mother was at the salon, thank God. I couldn't have handled seeing either of them.

My friend ran her hands up and down my arms. "Then you have a baby. You'll be a great mom. But let's not get ahead of ourselves. What are the odds you're actually pregnant? You said you haven't even been having sex, which is definitely a prerequisite. You probably have an ulcer or something."

"I hope so." Which seemed like a twisted thing to wish for but it would be highly preferable over bringing a baby into the whole visa situation. It wasn't that I didn't want a baby, because I really, really did. Eventually. But the timing utterly sucked.

"I have the test in my purse. Let's go in your bathroom."

Savannah peeled off her coat and hung it up. She glanced around. "Nice apartment. It looks like everything is almost ready for the party tonight."

"Michael's mother is a force of nature. She did the majority of the work." I was still hurt my own mother had decided not to attend. It didn't exactly reassure me that I would be returning to her less than open arms if I had to go back to England.

"I couldn't get a sitter, so I'm bringing Sully. We probably won't stay long. Cocktails parties with a baby are not ideal."

"I totally understand." I shut the bedroom door behind us and locked it. I held my hand out. "Okay, give me this damn thing."

She pulled a brown bag out of her purse and handed it to me.

"Here goes nothing." I took a deep breath and went into the bathroom.

The directions were straightforward and after washing my hands I let Savannah into the bathroom. "I'm sure it will be negative. I think this is stress." Eighty-five percent of me felt that way. The other fifteen percent was convinced I was pregnant. "We used condoms and I don't remember any slipups."

"Then I'm sure it will be negative." She tucked her red hair behind her ears. "But if it's positive, focus on the end game. You'll have a baby and that's the best thing in the world, trust me, I know. Plus, you have a great guy and you're going to have an amazing house."

"If our offer is accepted. We haven't heard back from the agent yet." Making an offer on the brownstone was super impulsive given our complicated-as-fuck lives but I hadn't been able to resist. It was just perfect.

I paced back and forth, avoiding the teak vanity. "You look first. I can't take it."

There was a pause, then Savannah said, "Do you want me to tell you the result?"

I squeezed my eyes shut. Did I? Yes. I had to know. "Give it to me straight."

"You're pregnant."

Somehow in my panicked state I wasn't sure if there had been a "not" in her sentence. "Wait, what? I'm not pregnant or I'm pregnant?"

"You *are* pregnant. The test is positive."

Everything inside me went hot. I felt a rush of heat up into my cheeks and I got a little lightheaded. Holy shit. I was going to be a mum. It was utterly terrifying but it was also, well, exciting. A tiny human. Made by me and Michael.

At least I could guarantee that he wasn't going to be upset.

"I guess it's not an ulcer," I said in an attempt at a joke.

"Are you okay?" Savannah asked, worried. She came over and took my hands. "I know this is a shock."

I nodded and took a deep breath. "I'm okay. I'm fine. I'm actually, well, happy. About the baby, I mean. But it's really bad timing."

Worst timing ever actually.

"Babies don't give a flip about timing." She gave me a grin. "Oh my God, I'm so happy for you! Sully will have a buddy!"

"If I'm not tossed out of the US." Right now though, I couldn't even think about that. I just wanted to wander around in wonderment and awe that I was having a baby.

"That's what lawyers are for and Michael will be all over this now that you're pregnant."

"I don't think I should tell him before the party." I wasn't going to tell him until after we had our "are we staying together or not" conversation. I needed to know that he cared about me. Maybe he didn't love me yet, but I needed to know he had feelings for me that went beyond friendship and appreciation for our great sex life.

"Good call. That would throw him off his social game. He would want to tell everyone and truthfully, you're so early in the pregnancy, you should wait a couple months before telling everyone you know."

She had a fair point but the thought of miscarrying made me feel fiercely protective of my budding zygote. I ran my hand over my stomach. "I don't think he could resist announcing it tonight if I told him. Michael is going to be thrilled."

He was going to be over the moon.

Because he wanted a baby really badly.

A sudden unwelcome and hideously ugly thought popped into my head.

Would he do anything to have a baby?

Gloria's words at lunch came back to me. Check the condoms for holes.

He wouldn't. There was no way he would do something so shady.

No one would do that. Certainly not Michael.

Or would he?

I tossed the pregnancy test into the wastebasket and took the empty box and shoved it under the sink under a towel.

Time to celebrate a fake engagement while hiding a very real pregnancy.

This could get interesting.

"CONGRATULATIONS," my friend Jim said to me, shaking my hand and clapping me on the shoulder.

"Thanks, man, I'm a lucky guy."

"I'll say. Don't punch me but your fiancée is hot."

"She's very hot and she would never give you the time I day." I grinned at Jim.

"Dick. Though you're right." He shrugged. "I have a shitty personality."

That made me laugh.

It was probably the fortieth time I'd had this kind of exchange and you know? It wasn't getting old. The steady stream of my friends and family coming over to give their good wishes had been awesome. It was short notice, most of these people had never met Felicia, and yet they had turned out to be happy for me.

Yep. I meant it wholeheartedly when I said I was a lucky guy.

The room was filled with people, music, and food stations. I hadn't even known this many people could fit in my apartment, let alone with a Christmas tree and half a dozen high-top tables. I didn't have eyes on Felicia right then because there were just too many people. The last I'd seen her she was introducing me to her friend Leah and Leah's fiancé, Grant. They'd both seemed like great people, very friendly, and they seemed genuinely happy for Felicia.

My sister hadn't been able to make it from California, but other than that, everyone I truly cared about was in the room.

"Does Felicia have a sister?" Jim asked as my cousin Brent came up with a drink in his hand.

"No, she does not." Not that I was aware of anyway.

"Are any of her friends single?"

"Dude, my fiancée is not your personal matchmaker. Have either of you seen Sean?" My brother wasn't there yet and it was pissing me off.

"Nope. Good eats, man. Great party." Brent sipped his drink. "I didn't think you'd ever get married again, to be honest."

"Why? I've never had anything against marriage."

"You were always a workaholic. I figured you'd just stay single and have lots of sex with random women, living the life we all wish we could have."

"Excuse me?" Brent's wife, Kathryn, appeared behind him.

He choked on his drink. "Nothing."

"You're an asshole, Brent," was her response. She rubbed her temples. "Michael, any chance you have something for a headache? It's been brewing all day and now it's really gotten bad. I don't have any aspirin in this damn clutch." She displayed her tiny purse.

"Sure. Let me go grab you some." I handed Brent my empty glass. "I'd have a headache every night if I was married to this prick."

"Ha-ha, you're fucking hilarious." Brent made a face.

"For the record," Kathryn said as I shifted away from them.

"You had years before we met to have lots of sex with random women and you didn't, so what does that tell you?"

Ouch. That was an unpleasant truth bomb for Brent.

It was slow progress across the apartment, people greeting and commenting to me as I went. Despite the fact that we had the visa process looming over us, I was really damn happy. I wanted to marry Felicia and none of what I was saying about her was fake. I was telling all my friends and family she was witty, intelligent, and giving. What I wasn't telling them was that she was intriguing, sexy as fuck, and going to keep me on my toes for the rest of my life.

This was not a trial run or a wait-and-see for me.

After everyone left I was going to tell her I'd fallen in love with her.

I wanted her to stay in New York and wait out the application process.

In our new home if we got the townhouse. I was still waiting to hear from Krisha.

Felicia was standing in the kitchen talking to my mother. I was glad they seemed to get along. The day had been crazy intense but Felicia did seem to be feeling better than the day before.

My phone buzzed in my pocket, so I pulled it out from habit. I wasn't on call but it was habit to be accessible.

It was a text from Krisha.

Your offer was accepted. Congratulations.

Holy shit, we'd bought a house.

If you had asked me six weeks ago if I'd be buying an enormous townhouse on the Upper West Side, I would have said you were crazy. But apparently, I was the crazy one because now I was about to own a four-million-dollar piece of Manhattan.

I guess I'd done crazier things than buy only the second property I looked at. Like, for example, getting engaged to a woman I barely knew. Who had catfished me.

There was a bizarre beginning to a love story.

The thought made me grin as I went into the bathroom and rooted around. I didn't know where anything was anymore. Felicia

FORTY DAY FIANCÉ   183

had moved her stuff in and rearranged all of mine under the guise of making room for her. I thought it had more to do with her stubbornly preferring her system of what went where but I didn't really care that much. I found a bottle of acetaminophen and twisted the cap. The whole thing tilted sideways and the bottle shot out of my hand, across the countertop, and down onto the floor, spilling pills everywhere.

"Shit." I bent down and fished the half-spilled bottle off the floor. Picking up pills on the floor I tossed them in the wastebasket.

I had already pulled my hand away when I processed the fact that I had seen something odd in the trash. Taking a second look, I confirmed it. A pregnancy test. I pulled it out and studied the results.

A positive pregnancy test.

Holy shit.

Felicia was pregnant. She did not have an ulcer.

She was having our baby.

I grinned. Merry Christmas to me.

I was getting everything I'd ever wanted all in one perfect package.

When I went back to the party, searching out Kathryn to give her the pills, I felt almost drunk with happiness, even though I'd only had one drink. Having a fiancée, soon a new home, with a baby on the way was the best buzz I'd ever had. I guess the term was punch drunk. That was me. Fucking on top of the world.

My brother was standing by the front door, arguing with a woman I'd never met. A girlfriend? I went over to greet him. "Where the hell have you been?" I asked him. "You're like an hour late."

"I got stuck in your fucking elevator! Don't you ever look at your phone?"

"It's my engagement party. I'm not staring at my phone." But I pulled it out and frowned. I had received the text from Krisha, but nothing from Sean. "I don't even have a text from you."

"That's because I told you texting from elevators is dicey," the woman said, giving Sean an icy stare. "Like it would have killed you just to push the help button?"

This date clearly wasn't going well. I held my hand out to her. "I'm Michael, by the way."

She took my hand. "Isla. Nice to meet you. I've heard great things about you from Felicia. Your brother, on the other hand, is an asshole."

"I can verify that," I said.

"Shut up," Sean said to me. He shot a look at Isla. "Well, nice meeting you. And yes, I mean that sarcastically. I'm going to get a drink." He clapped my shoulder. "Congratulations, you crazy son of a bitch. I wish you a lifetime of happiness and hope you never find yourself tied to your bed with your balls glued to your thighs."

He handed his coat to the attendant we'd hired to store coats in Felicia's half-empty closet and beelined for the booze.

"What the hell was that about?" I asked Isla, who I now realized was not Sean's date, but Felicia's friend.

"We had the misfortune of stepping onto the elevator at the same time." She rolled her eyes. "We were stuck for exactly eight minutes. Eight minutes of my life I'll never get back. And what is he talking about? Ball glueing? What the hell?"

"He thinks Felicia is probably a psychopath who will torture and stalk me for the rest of my life if things don't work out. This is based on nothing other than the fact that she was messaging me as Savannah initially."

"Ah. He does seem like the suspicious type, though I am too, so I can't find fault with that or his concerns. But I'm not a drama queen. That was a dramatic statement."

That made me laugh. "He is a drama queen." I reached out to take her coat. "Can I get you a drink?" I held up my closed fist. "I need to make an aspirin delivery to a friend with a headache but after that I can grab you whatever you want."

"Thanks, but I'll be fine. I see Felicia."

I nodded. "Thanks for coming."

She shot me a look that made me wonder if she knew Felicia

was pregnant. No. Felicia wouldn't tell all her friends before she told me, would she? It seemed like I should be the first to know.

I delivered the pills to Kathryn, who took them eagerly, and went to find my fiancée. I was bursting with the knowledge of her pregnancy. I needed to pull her into our bedroom and tell her I knew. Which made me wonder why she hadn't told me? Maybe she wasn't happy about it. Or maybe it was just the timing with the party. I was pretty certain that test hadn't been in the wastebasket the day before.

Felicia was standing with a group of her friends. She didn't look unhappy. She still looked pale but she was smiling and laughing.

"I'm sorry to interrupt," I said, "but I have some news."

Felicia started and her cheeks turned pink. "What's that?"

"We got the townhouse. They accepted our offer."

"What? They didn't even counter?"

"No, they just accepted it. It was a fair offer." I took her hand and lifted it to my mouth. "Merry Christmas, Felicia. We have a new house."

"Oh my God," she breathed. "That beautiful home is ours?"

I nodded. "All ours. We're going to need to buy some furniture. It's four thousand square feet."

"Woo hoo!" Savannah clapped her hands and moved her hands like she was raising the roof. "Congratulations, you guys!"

"Thanks, Savannah." It was amusing to me now that I had ever put her face to Felicia's words. Savannah in person was nothing like Felicia.

A guy who looked like he was in his mid-twenties and covered in tattoos, approached with a baby, who was crying hot angry tears. "We're going to have to go, babe," he said. "He's losing it."

This was the guy Savannah had been in love with when she went to dinner with me? He had to be damn near twenty years younger than me. Jesus. I owed him and his tats a huge thank you. If he hadn't been on the fringes, things might have turned out differently and I was really fucking happy with the way they had turned out.

I held out my hand. "Thanks for coming, we appreciate it. I'm Michael, by the way. You must be Maddox. It's great to meet you."

Maddox shook my hand. "Nice to meet you too. Congrats. Felicia's an awesome person."

I touched the baby's arm. He gave me a sketched-out look. "Hey, it's okay, buddy. You're going home."

He was stretching out his arms for Savannah, but she was dodging him. "This is horrible. I can't take him. He wants to nurse and I cut him off a week ago. If I take him, he'll face plant into my chest and cry until he passes out."

Maddox was turning so that Sully couldn't see his mother, cuddling and bouncing him. The baby had reached full-on screaming now, his face red, a line of snot running out of his nose onto his lip. "You can't give in, babe, or we'll just be teaching him he gets what he wants if he kicks up enough of a fuss. He's not even hungry, he just ate."

"I know, it's just my heart hurts." Savannah turned quickly away from the sight of her crying son. "I'll go get our coats."

Maddox looked at me and shrugged. He ran a reassuring hand over the baby's head and swayed with him. "He's a boob man. Can you blame him?"

That made me laugh. "No, not at all."

Once Maddox had left I turned my attention back to Felicia. She was repeatedly taking deep breaths like she might get sick. "What's wrong?"

"Babies are a lot of work, aren't they? Oh God..."

For a second I thought she was going to faint. I grabbed her shoulders hard to keep her from going down, but she rallied. There was fifty people milling in my apartment all around us but I couldn't stop myself from demanding, "You're pregnant, aren't you?"

Her eyes widened but she just nodded. "Can we please go in the bedroom? It's really hot in here."

"Of course." I led her down the hall, my arm wrapped around her shoulders as she leaned on me.

I heard Brent say, "Dude, sneaking off to the bedroom? Wait until everyone leaves, geez."

My cousin was an idiot. But it probably didn't look that great from the perspective of everyone in the living room. I flipped Brent off over my shoulder. He laughed.

"Everyone thinks we're off to shag, don't they?" Felicia asked with a weak smile as she sat on the edge of the bed.

"Yep. Joke's on them. We never shag."

She laughed. "The irony is tremendous. We don't shag and yet, I'm pregnant. But we did shag before. Quite well and more than once. "

I pushed her hair off her forehead. She was clammy. "Do you want to lie down?"

She started to, then grabbed my arm and hauled herself back up. "No, that was worse. That made me really dizzy. Is this what being pregnant is like? Everyone always looks so damn perky posing with their bumps. I feel like complete and utter ass."

"It's my understanding it's different for everyone. Even sometimes from pregnancy to pregnancy."

She eyed me. "You don't seem surprised by this news."

"I am very surprised. I know you haven't been feeling well, but I didn't think you could actually be pregnant. But I came in here half an hour ago to get aspirin for my cousin's wife and found the pregnancy test. I think I'm still in shock." I stood in front of her, my hands in the pockets of my suit pants.

"Me too." She took more small breaths and rubbed her stomach. "It's like my innards are crawling up my throat."

"Do you want me to help you out of your dress?"

"That's what got us into this in the first place," she said, dryly. "Besides, I can't exactly mingle with our guests in my joggers and an enormous sweatshirt."

"You don't have to go out there if you don't want to. I'll tell everyone you're sick." It wasn't ideal but I didn't want her fainting at our engagement party.

"No, it's fine. I can manage another hour. I think seeing Sully screaming just freaked me out on top of the nausea."

"Stick by me. I'll get you out if you need to throw up or something."

She nodded and reached for my hand. "Help me up, please. By the way, your brother made quite the impression on Isla. She spent ten minutes ranting about how horrid he is."

"I think the feeling was mutual." I hauled her off the bed.

"They are both a couple of charmers." Felicia blew out a breath and reached up with a shaky hand to smooth her hair back. "I guess we can talk about the elephant in the room later?"

"The baby?" I asked. "Yes, but in case you need reassurance, I'm very happy. I know the timing is terrible, but I'm excited to start a family with you."

She nodded but didn't respond.

I wanted to tell her that I loved her but when I tried to make eye contact she glanced away.

Yep. Bad fucking timing all the way around.

A bad feeling kicked me in the gut.

But I ignored it and went back to our party.

SEVENTEEN

BY THE END of the night, I was exhausted. Like the kind of fatigue where walking across the room feels like it might kill you. I wasn't sure if it was being pregnant or the party or the stress of impending deportment, but I felt like total ass. Any one of those alone would have been enough to droop my sails, but the trio together was like being hit by a truck.

Without bothering to put them away (which would normally drive me bonkers) I kicked off my Louboutins and reached behind me to unzip my dress. I couldn't reach the damn zipper. "Michael!" I yelled, in a burst of frustration.

He appeared in the doorway of my closet in a towel, as if he'd been about to step into the shower. "What's wrong?" he asked, looking at me like he wasn't sure if he should grab me or call 911.

"Nothing. I can't get this dress off." I dropped my hands. "I'm going to scream if I can't be in bed in the next three minutes."

He walked into the closet and unzipped the dress. He held my hand while I stepped out of it. "Should I hang it up?" he asked.

"I don't give a shit, honestly." Initially I'd been happy about the baby, about the townhouse, but as the night wore on I had to admit I'd been expecting some kind of speech or declaration of his love from Michael.

We had a week before my visa expired and I'd got it in my head that this would be the night we discussed if this was going to stick or not. I'd thought he would either say something publicly or we could have a conversation about it without him knowing about the baby. I didn't want him to be with me solely because of a pregnancy. But the devious bastard had somehow spotted the test. Not that I'd hid it particularly well in my panicked state, but still.

He was going to push to marry me now, I knew that. Yet I still had no clue how he actually felt about me. Plus, there was a little concern that kept popping up in my head.

"How do you think I got pregnant?" I asked as I pulled open a drawer and pulled out an oversized T-shirt. I wanted to sleep in cotton.

He gave me a grin. "Want me to show you? I can give you a hands-on demonstration."

"I'd rather sleep for a week straight but thanks for the kind offer."

Michael's towel knot slipped and he held it together with his fist. "If you were feeling better, I'd think you made my towel slip with your mind. You are a witch, remember?"

I wasn't in the mood for witty banter. "I'm serious. How did I get pregnant? We used condoms."

"They're not foolproof."

"You didn't do this on purpose, did you?" I asked, just needing to address the issue straightaway.

"What?" To his credit, he looked astonished. "Why the fuck would you ask that? No, of course not."

"Your mother told me at lunch I should check the condoms to make sure you hadn't poked holes in them. She said that's how much you want a baby."

His nostrils flared. He rubbed his jaw. His eyes were angry. "My mother has no business talking about my sex life. Though I doubt she was actually serious. It sounds like she was joking. But why would you think for one second I would do something that manipulative and fucking psycho?"

He was angrier than I expected. "I don't know. Maybe because you've made it very clear from the beginning what you want from me is a baby." I pulled the shirt on over my head.

Michael was just staring at me, his jaw working.

"You can't deny it. Those were the terms. You got me a green card, I would make you a dad."

"That is really oversimplifying what we agreed to. Why don't you just go to bed? We can talk about this tomorrow. Today was a long day."

I wasn't sure what he was supposed to do or if I was overreacting but to me his tone sounded condescending and that just was the perfect exclamation point on the whole situation. It was like everything I'd been worried about with another older man right there in front of me. Daddy knows best. Damn. Ignoring the hand he held out for me I just shifted past him out of the closet and went to the bedroom. It seemed to take all of my energy to even climb up onto the mattress.

Michael didn't follow me and that was fine with me.

I thought I would have trouble falling asleep but the day caught up me with. I was out instantly, though my last thought was that I was having a baby.

Holy shit.

THE APARTMENT WAS a disaster of dirty glasses and plates, overflowing trash receptacles, and linen napkins the caterers were supposed to pick up in three days' time, the day after Christmas. It matched my mood as I pulled blankets and a pillow out of my closet in the bedroom. Chaos and confusion. Felicia was already asleep. I took the bedding to the couch, trying to process how I was feeling. I was really damn upset that she thought I was capable of such a dick move as to get her pregnant on purpose.

But I wasn't going to explode our whole relationship over that. I just figured she needed rest and time and I needed to let her have that. But there was no denying I was pissed. And excited. And concerned.

We would have a real conversation the next day and everything would be resolved. It would be fine. Hell, fucking awesome.

It had to be.

After turning off the Christmas tree lights, I watched TV until three in the morning, tossing and turning on the couch, before finally falling asleep. I woke up to Felicia shaking me.

"What? What's wrong?" The shaking was aggressive. I rubbed my forehead and eyes. "What time is it?"

"I have no idea. Why are you sleeping on the couch?"

"Because I thought you needed a good night's sleep. I didn't want to disturb you. And I was pissed off," I said. I wasn't about to deny that.

She was leaning over me, her dark hair falling over her face. She looked as angry as I'd felt the night before. I waited for her to say something. When she didn't I closed my eyes again. It felt like I'd been asleep for an hour, tops.

"Michael!" She shook me again.

"What?" I sighed and forced my eyes open again. God, I hated mornings.

"Can we please talk?" She sat down in the chair across from me, pulling her legs up under the T-shirt she was wearing.

"How are you feeling?" I asked, assessing her color. She looked a lot better.

"I feel okay. I slept hard." Then without preamble, she said, "What are we going to do?"

I sat up, swinging my feet around to the floor. "About what?" I knew she meant everything, but maybe we could start with one specific portion of the overall issue.

"Don't be daft. About the visa. We're supposed to be deciding this week if we stay together or not."

That wasn't already a guarantee?

Fuck. I needed coffee. "Let me start the coffee. Do you want me to make you tea?"

"Yes. But do you want to be with me or not?"

I was halfway to standing. I reached out and squeezed her knee. "Sweetheart, I just bought a four-million-dollar townhouse for you. I thought it was obvious I wanted to be with you. Besides, I never would have agreed to a party with all my family and friends present if I wasn't already sure about my feelings."

She put her chin on her knees. "But you didn't say anything last night at the party. There was no toast, or declaration of your feelings."

Oh, God. I'd stepped into that trap? "I didn't think you were the grand gesture type of woman. I'm sorry if I disappointed you." I was. "Besides, I'd just found out about the pregnancy and I had a lot of shit running through my head. I didn't know you needed a speech."

She'd been with me until I added the last sentence, then she gasped and shot me a frown. "I didn't need a *speech*, don't make me sound like a twat."

On that note, I went to the kitchen and took a mug down out of the cabinet. I put it under my coffeemaker and hit the button. I rustled around for tea in a drawer. She'd moved in and taken up at least three drawers with tea crap. I hadn't even complained. I'd just let her. She'd taken over my life and I had let her and why? Because I wanted this relationship.

If she couldn't see that, I wasn't sure what in the hell else I was supposed to do to prove it. Obviously make a toast but not take it so far that it was a speech. Find that muddy line and I'd give you a thousand bucks.

My back was still to her but I asked, "What is it *you* want to do about the visa, Felicia?" I had a feeling I wasn't going to like her answer.

"I'm going back to England."

I looked at her over my shoulder as I got a teacup down for her. "Just like that? No discussion, no input from me?"

She nodded. "It's my decision."

That pissed me off. Really pissed me off. "Except now you're having my baby. So it's not just your decision. I'm the father. I have a say, too." A baby. What I desperately wanted. A child to love and raise. We were having a baby and here she was talking about taking my flesh and blood away from me? Not happening.

She recoiled from the sound of anger in my voice. "I didn't say I was going forever. Just while I wait for the fiancée visa."

That mollified me slightly. "Not spousal?"

She shook her head.

"What if I don't want you to go? Not just because of the baby but because I don't want to be without you."

"It's the right thing to do," she said. "Legally."

"Fuck legally. Is that what you want? To be apart from me?" I picked up my coffee mug and took a big swallow, burning the fuck out of my tongue. "Ow, shit." I set the mug back down, hard, splashing liquid over the back of my hand.

"No, I don't want to be away from you. But we have to be logical because I *am* pregnant. I need to not screw this up."

"I... me... where is the *we* in this?"

She eyed me. "So what would you have me do?"

"Marry me and stay here."

"Why should I marry you, Michael?" she asked, her voice soft and contemplative.

Because I loved her. Because I'd been intrigued by her since the first minute I'd met her. But if she didn't want to marry me, and she wanted to leave, I wasn't sure now was the right time to tell her how I felt.

Damn it, I wished I'd told her sooner.

I made her tea and wished I could read her mind. I didn't know the answer she was fishing for. I was failing the pop quiz and I hated that. "Because we're having a baby and I don't want to risk you getting stuck on another continent for who knows how long."

She made a sound of frustration and dropped her feet to the floor. "No. That is never a good reason to get married."

Wrong answer, then. Okay, I'd go with choice B. "Because we're great together." I brought the tea over to her and set it on the coffee table. "Because from the minute I found out you were the woman I'd been talking to, I knew we had a connection."

She just shook her head slowly like I'd failed again.

"What do you want me to say?" I asked, frustrated.

"I want you to tell me that you love me."

Fuck. I'd waited too long. I'd wanted it to be the right moment and now I'd waited too long and everything was all kinds of fucked up. "I love you, Felicia. I do. Trust me."

"I don't want you to say it now because I *asked* you to!" She stood up and took her tea and left the living room.

"That is not why I said it. Where are you going?"

"To England!"

"Seriously? When?" That infuriated me. "You're just going to walk out before we even discuss this any further?"

"There is nothing to discuss. I'm going to get a flight for as soon as possible."

She couldn't be serious. Just like that? It was so abrupt and *wrong*. "There are a million things to discuss." That she would just dismiss me and our relationship was not cool. "If you book a flight today, it's over, Felicia. I'm not kidding. You don't get to walk out like that."

She stopped in the hallway and turned slowly. "You don't get to throw out ultimatums. I feel like you need to retract that statement."

She sounded icy cold, which annoyed me even further. I was the one getting done dirty. Hadn't she thrown out an ultimatum?

"No," I said and it wasn't even totally out of stubbornness. "You can't make life-altering decisions without me and expect I'm just going to be cool with it. By the way, you accused me of poking holes in a fucking condom and I'm supposed to just be fine with that but I can't be upset with you moving across the ocean?"

Her answer was to walk into our bedroom and slam the door shut.

I sipped my coffee and stewed, staring at the unlit Christmas tree. My life had gone from bland to amazing to shit all in less than forty days. That had to be a record.

My anger was preventing me from being heartbroken at the moment, but I knew that was going to show up later like a punch in the eye.

Wandering through the mess of high-top tables and chairs, I found the bar station.

Uncapping the whiskey, I splashed some in my coffee.

I looked at the Christmas gift I'd wrapped and put under the tree for Felicia and added more whiskey.

I BEGGED off Christmas Eve dinner out with my parents by saying Felicia and I were exhausted from the engagement party. They bought it. Sean didn't.

He showed up and found me sitting alone in a dark apartment, surrounded by the catering crap. I was eating leftover crab puffs and getting filthy, stinking drunk.

"Dude," he said when he opened the door to my apartment and came in. "You're actually breaking my heart. This is pathetic."

I didn't really care. "Want a drink?"

"Yes." He walked into the living room. "Now explain to me why you're drinking alone in the dark twenty-four hours after your engagement party?"

"We had a fight and Felicia's going back to England." Then I frowned. "You know what? It wasn't even a fight. She just decided she's going back."

"So the 'immersion dating while living together' experiment didn't work out?"

I shrugged. My chest hurt. It was like someone had reached into my ribcage and pulled my heart out with their bare hands. "I thought it did. I thought she wanted to be with me but she wanted to go back to England and wait for the official fiancée visa to go through before coming back. Because she doesn't have a permanent visa."

"Ah, now it all makes sense." Sean sat down with a heavy sigh and looked around at the cluttered coffee table. "Jesus, look at this place. Well, that doesn't sound like a breakup to me. She just wanted to make sure nothing went wrong with the application process. I can't fault her for that."

"She's pregnant." I tossed back the rest of my bourbon in one hot, burning swallow.

"Oh, shit."

"I put an offer on a townhouse two days ago. Yesterday she finds out she's pregnant. Today she says she's going to England. It's a big fucking mess."

"That visa will come through in a couple of months. She'll be back here way before the baby is born. Don't stress out. It will work out."

"Except that she accused me of getting her pregnant on purpose and said I should have made a speech at the party saying I love her. No, not a speech. A declaration of love. Then I said if she left against my wishes I was done with our relationship." I rubbed my forehead. "It fucking went off the rails, man."

"Do you love her?" he asked.

"Yes," I said without hesitation. "I know you thinks it's crazy, but I love her, Sean. I look at her and I can't even imagine a future without her in it. She makes me feel... *fierce*."

"Fierce, like Beyonce?" Sean asked. "I don't get it."

I shot him a glare. "No, you asshole. Fierce like fiercely protective and fiercely in love and fiercely passionate." I gave a snort and stood up to get more booze. "Like Beyonce. Go fuck yourself."

"What? I don't know. But okay, I get it now." Sean joined me at the bar station. "These glasses are all dirty. You're drinking out of a dirty glass. That's disgusting."

"No, I'm not that drunk. I got it out of the kitchen."

He went into the kitchen and retrieved one for himself off of the open shelving. He also came back with a garbage bag.

"What's that for?"

"All these napkins lying around. It's nasty, I can't stand it." He poured himself a drink and snapped open the garbage bag.

I sat back down heavily and watched him collecting linen napkins from all over the room and tossing them in the bag.

"Leave that by the door," I said. "The caterer is picking up all that shit on the twenty-sixth."

"Sure. Okay, let's start at the beginning. Did you get her pregnant on purpose?"

"No, what the fuck? I would never do something like that." My own brother thought I was capable of knocking up someone on purpose? That was just messed up.

"I'm just checking. You were planning to hire a surrogate. I mean, you wanted a baby, bad. It might have been tempting to put the condom on after a little tip action."

"You're an asshole. No, I didn't do that. I'm not seventeen. And never say 'tip action' in front of me again." I ate another crab puff. "There's a bunch of leftovers in the fridge if you're hungry."

"No offense, but that wasn't the best catering."

"Okay, Chef Dickhead. You try to book a caterer on ten days' notice at the holidays." They tasted fine to me but I was drunk.

"Did she harp on the condom thing or did she believe you after you told her you did not do that."

"I don't know if she believed me but she let it go."

"I don't think you should end your relationship because she had what is frankly a legitimate question considering the length of time you've known each other."

"That is not technically why we broke up."

"Then why did you break up?" Sean dumped the bag by the door and washed his hands vigorously in the kitchen sink. "That was fucking disgusting."

"I'm not really exactly sure why we broke up," I said. "Maybe because she's taking my baby to England against my wishes. Or maybe because I never told her I love her. I'm not exactly sure at this point."

"You're fucking loaded."

I nodded. "Yes, I am. I've been drinking since ten this morning."

"I can tell. When is she going to England?"

"Tomorrow. She texted me her flight information earlier."

"She's flying on Christmas Day? Damn. She really wants away from you."

I kicked his leg. Hard. "What did you do to Isla, by the way? You made a very negative impression on her."

He gave a snort. "The feeling was mutual. She's one of those man-haters. I couldn't say anything without her getting offended."

"Huh," I said, because I didn't really care. "I'm going to drunk text Felicia later and make it worse, aren't I?" I asked.

"No. Because I'm taking you back to my apartment and taking your phone away from you."

"Good. Thanks, bro. I love you."

"Eat another lousy crab puff and drink some water."

EIGHTEEN

"I THINK you need to just stop and think this through for a minute," Isla said to me on the phone, while I paced in the gate area, pulling my rolling bag behind me.

I was flying back to England on Christmas Day because the airfare had been substantially cheaper. It was depressing as hell, but at the same time, I had wanted to escape. Put an ocean between me and my heartache and confusion. "Think what through? I have one week before my visa expires."

"That's seven days from now. Hang out for a few days, make sure you've approached this from every angle, let your emotions even out. Talk to Michael..."

That made my stomach tighten. "He broke up with me. I'm not sure what there is to talk about. He said if I walked out, we were done."

"There is always something to talk about after a fight. That's what this was. A fight. You can't just end it without at least having a rational conversation."

I blew my air out of my eyes and stopped pacing. "You of all people should be supporting me right now. He gave me an ultimatum. No one should do that to someone else."

"I totally agree. But he just found out you're pregnant and then you said you're going back to England, which if we're being honest here is a bit of an ultimatum in its own right. Maybe you both over-reacted. Your relationship has been going at warp speed since day one. Slow it down and talk."

"He's never once said he loved me," I told her. "Well. Once. After I told him to tell me and he did. God, worst proclamation of love ever."

"Is he supposed to love you?" she asked. "Can he just care about you a lot and be *falling* in love with you? Again, it hasn't been that long."

"I love *him*." She was starting to irritate me.

"Yeah, but, and don't take this the wrong way, but you don't exactly wear your heart on your sleeve. You're very hard to read."

I wrinkled my nose. "How exactly am I not supposed to take that the wrong way? Look, I told myself not to fall in love with him until I knew he was in love with me, so I wouldn't get hurt. But what did I do? Oh, I fell in love with him. Like, instantly. Probably within days if I'm being honest with myself. I'm hopeless."

"I feel like you're bringing your past relationship trust issues into this. You don't trust his feelings."

I plopped down on a hard plastic chair and pulled my suitcase between my legs. She was right. I knew she was right. How annoying was that? "I don't know if it's me he wants or the baby. I wish we'd talked before I took the test."

"That ship has sailed, babe. You can't go back. You have to decide if you want to fight for this relationship or not."

"I don't know what to do." I rubbed my temple. "I'm trying to not get in trouble with American immigration and do the right thing for both me and my baby. I'm trying to be mature."

"The mature thing to do is to call your fiancé. He is your legit fiancé, by the way. It was written all over his face at the party. He's into you. Also, given what a prick his brother is, Michael seems to be a really nice guy."

I groaned. "This is such a mess. How did this happen?"

"It happened because of a million weird little things. Like you talking to him as Savannah. Like him having clothes he needed you to sell. You leaving your tablet and group texting you wanted to shag him. You failing to mail your application."

"That was the mailman's fault." It wasn't really, because ultimately the buck stopped with me, but I was feeling a little bruised at the moment.

The overhead speaker announced boarding for my flight to Heathrow.

"That's not my point. My point is that maybe your relationship was meant to be. You got pregnant basically your first night together. Maybe this is all the way it's supposed to be."

That made me wonder who had kidnapped and brainwashed Isla. That was not her approach to love or hell, life. "Who are you? Where is my friend Isla?"

She laughed. "Screw you."

"You sound like Savannah." It was unnerving. I relied on Isla to be the cynic in any given situation. I always used them both as outliers so that I could land somewhere in the middle.

"I just think sometimes you have to stop fighting against what is happening. Look, if I had to predict what was going to happen thirty-five days ago, I would have said it wouldn't have lasted two days. That you'd both walk away hating each other, but that is clearly not the case."

I chewed my lip. I didn't know what to do. "My plane is boarding, I have to go."

"Okay. Be safe. Text me when you land."

"I will. And... thanks, Isla."

"I'll send you my bill."

That made me laugh, despite wanting to cry. We ended the call and I got in line to board.

"CAN YOU GO ANY FASTER?" I asked the cab driver.

He just rolled his eyes at me in the rearview mirror.

We were pulling into JFK but I was eyeing the time on my phone with serious impatience.

When I'd woken up with a massive hangover and a text from Felicia asking me to call her when I was up, I'd decided this had to happen in person. Not over the phone. Not in a text. But face-to-face. I needed to tell her that I loved her in a way that she believed me.

So I'd bought a seat on her flight to London.

I didn't want five rushed minutes at the airport.

I had two weeks.

It was the most time off work I could manage on such short notice and a week of that was because of the holidays, thank God. But it was a start.

If I actually made my flight.

As the cab pulled up in front of the airline I threw money at the driver and hopped out. My head was still throbbing and I had no idea what I had actually packed. I'd just opened drawers and thrown shit in there. None of that mattered. What mattered was getting to the woman I loved.

Using the kiosk, I checked in and then went to the security line. It wasn't horrible, given it was Christmas Day, but it was long enough to make me bounce back and forth on the balls of my feet.

"Would you mind if I went ahead of you?" I asked the woman in front of me. "I'm late for my flight."

"That's not my problem," she said, with a frown. "You should have left on time."

The Christmas spirit apparently didn't apply to the security line at JFK.

I waited, repeatedly checking the time on my phone, the line moving with zero sense of urgency. Finally, I got to the front. I kicked my shoes off, threw my bag on the belt, and went through the body scan.

"Someone's in a hurry," the TSA officer said.

She gave me a smile though, which was reassuring I wasn't

about to get pulled aside and frisked. "If I miss this flight, my relationship is over."

"Ah, I see." She jerked her thumb. "Go get your stuff. You're clear."

"Thank you and Merry Christmas." I grabbed my bag and scanned the signs, trying to figure out which way to go, breaking out into a jog.

"You need a ride?" A guy who looked in his fifties pulled up alongside me in a cart. "You look like you're in a hurry."

"I am." I jumped up onto the cart and gave him my gate number. "I need to get on this flight and convince the woman I love, the mother of my child, that we should get married."

He eyed me, curious. "No shit? Well, hold on to your butt, let's go get her."

The cart leaped forward and I grabbed on to the rail. We were flying through the airport, dodging and weaving in and out of travelers. "That's some fine driving, sir, I'm impressed."

"I drove a Humvee in Iraq in the service. This isn't as fun."

"Thank you for your service," I said to him, grateful for his efforts then and now. We were eating up the gates. I glanced at the time. I had a text that said boarding had started. That gave me twenty minutes. I felt confident I was going to make it. "What's your name? I owe you big-time, man. Thank you, seriously."

"Name's Willie, and no problem," he said over his shoulder. "Who doesn't love a good love story? Especially on Christmas."

"I'm Michael. It's a pleasure to meet you."

We got to my gate and Willie just about popped a wheelie. I jumped off the cart. I handed him a hundred bucks and offered my hand for a shake. "Merry Christmas, Willie. Thanks again."

His eyes sparkled as he tucked the money in his shirt pocket. "You've got this, Mike."

I waved, turned, and realized my phone was ringing. Felicia. I scanned the boarding area as I put the phone to my ear. She wasn't there. Most of the waiting area was already empty.

"Hello?"

. . .

I SAT IN MY SEAT, foot bouncing, silently begging Michael to answer his phone. If he didn't, I wasn't sure I could stay on the plane. Isla was right. I had to talk to him.

"Hello?"

I closed my eyes in relief when he answered. "Michael, I'm sorry." My throat tightened. I didn't know what else to say, I had so many emotions overwhelming me. Where did I start?

"I'm sorry too. I didn't realize that I wasn't being clear in how I feel. I was trying not to pressure you and obviously, that was a huge mistake. I love you, Felicia, so damn much. I think you're amazing and I would want to marry you, baby or not."

Tears pricked at the back of my eyes. He sounded raw, sincere, urgent. "I'm such an idiot. I'm sitting on this plane and all I can think is that our fake engagement was the most real thing to ever happen to me. I love you too." I sighed, foot bouncing even more frantically. I glanced around. The plane was mostly full. It was now or never. "I'm getting off the plane."

I stood up and said, "Excuse me," to the woman next to me.

She barely moved her legs. I climbed over her, grateful I was wearing joggers and trainers.

"I'm in the boarding area," he said.

"What?" My heart started to pound. "What do you mean?" I grabbed my bag from the overhead and shoved past everyone pushing upstream like salmon. "Excuse me, sorry, I just forgot something."

The man of my dreams.

"I'm right outside your flight."

"How did you get there? You'll get arrested." Had he pulled a Love, Actually moment and jump over a barrier? Sexy, but dangerous as hell.

I jogged up the gateway.

"I bought a ticket."

Bursting through the doorway, I looked frantically around.

Michael was standing at the back of the boarding line. When he saw me he got out of line.

I ran to him.

He scooped me up and we had an epic airport moment. He twirled me around while I hugged him as tight as I possibly good.

"I love you," he said. "Let me prove it to you."

I kissed him. "You already have. And I love you too."

He kissed me back.

Then he set me down and got on one knee. My heart swelled.

"Felicia Hobbs, will you marry me? For real this time?"

I nodded frantically. "Yes. Absolutely."

He stood up and gave me a soft kiss. "I knew I loved you by day three," he said. "That first proposal was real."

"My yes was real, too. But I was trying to play hard to get."

He laughed. "Tell me about it. Do you know how much torture it has been to sleep next to you every night in those damn nightgowns and not touch you?"

"Trust me, I know." None of my logic made any sense now, but there had been some kind of point at the time. I glanced back at the line. The last person was boarding. "Are we getting on this flight?"

"We're either taking a flight tomorrow and going home for the night or you're going to join the mile-high club with me. I can't wait ten hours of traveling to have you, sweetheart. I've been waiting *forever*."

Given the way he was nuzzling my neck, I believed him. "We can fly tomorrow. Let's go home."

Home. I loved the sound of that.

Of course, when we got back to the flat I glanced around at the disaster of dirty dishes and abandoned rental tables. "God, I left you a first-class mess. I'm so sorry."

"It's both of our mess." Michael scooped me up into his arms. "But we can deal with it tomorrow. Today I just want to hold you and love you."

I hugged him tight. "I would like nothing more than that."

"But first, I have a gift for you." He went over to the Christmas tree and pulled out a gift.

The box was enormous, too big to be jewelry. That got me curious. "Michael, what did you do?"

Without hesitation, I sat on the sofa and ripped it open. It was an empty scrapbook and what looked like every tool needed to make the world's most blinged out memory book in the history of crafting.

"I didn't know what to get, so I got a variety."

One of everything. He'd gotten one of everything. It made me smile. "It's perfect, thank you. I'm going to get my craft on."

"Look inside that little box."

I pulled the lid off, anticipating jewelry. I was right. But this made me tear up. "It's a charm bracelet." With an engagement ring charm. "I had one as a girl and I loved it. It got lost when we had to move."

"I know. I called your mother and asked her what jewelry would be the right choice for you."

My heart was in my throat. I held the bracelet to my chest, vision blurred from my tears. "That is the sweetest thing anyone has ever done for me."

He kissed me softly. "I would do anything for you."

I was the luckiest woman in the history of ever. "Oh, I got something for you!" I turned and dug through my purse. I handed him a red envelope.

"Is this a gift card to a sex shop?" he asked, sounding absurdly hopeful. "I would love to see you in a leather corset."

That made me laugh. "No, you idiot. It's cooking lessons. For both of us, as a couple. We can't live on takeaway forever. We're having a child."

"That's a great idea." He did look genuinely pleased. "Time to grow up, huh?"

I nodded. "But that doesn't mean we can't get a leather corset for a sexy New Year's Eve."

Michael's eyes darkened. "Let's practice now."

"I'd love nothing more."

EPILOGUE

I PULLED the chair out for Felicia, who sat down with a sigh, her seven-months-pregnant belly a tight little ball stretching her summer black cotton dress. I was in awe every time I looked at her. My wife. Our baby girl, who we were planning to name Amelia.

I shook the Immigration interviewer's hand.

"We just need to ask a few questions."

"Sure, of course," I said. We were applying for the actual spousal license.

Felicia looked nervous, but I squeezed her knee to reassure her.

"Here's our scrapbook," she said, setting it down on the desk and pushing it toward him. "You can see our relationship has been documented from the beginning."

She'd worked hard on that and ironically, though it had started all for show, we both enjoyed looking at it now.

The dude barely glanced at it. I could instantly see Felicia get annoyed with him. I could read her facial expressions much better after living together on and off over the last six months. We'd done a lot of back-and-forth travel between the US and the UK but once her fiancée visa had been approved in April, we'd been living together full-time.

"My first set of questions are for Ms. Hobbs only. Are you a communist? Are you coming to the US to engage in espionage or act as a spy?"

She'd be a hot spy, I wasn't going to lie. I pictured her in black leather pants. Definitely a hot spy.

"No. And no."

"Are you intending to be a polygamist?"

"Hell no. I don't share well with others."

"Are you sexually intimate with Dr. Kincaid?" the man asked.

"Uh..." I glanced at Felicia, amused. "She's seven months pregnant. That's pretty obvious."

"I just need a yes or no answer from Ms. Hobbs."

"Yes." She gave me a wink as he wrote her response down. "Loads of sex."

Lots and lots of sex. The best sex I'd ever had.

"Just yes or no will suffice.

"What does Felicia do on Tuesdays?" he asked me, switching up the format.

"What?" The question was so random I drew a blank as to how to even answer that. "She works. At home. We have a new house and the ground level is her office space."

Then he went right back to Felicia. "Where did Dr. Kincaid attend college?"

"Stanford." Her voice was triumphant that she'd gotten it right.

"What was his first pet's name?"

"Bugsy. He had a pet rabbit at five years old."

Wow. I didn't even know she knew that. She'd clearly been talking to my mother again, which was fucking scary.

"Do you consider him to be a good driver?"

"A vehicle or a golf club?"

I laughed.

"Driving a car."

"No. He terrifies me every time we go to the Hamptons."

She was definitely a backseat driver.

"Who picks up the check when you go to dinner?"

"Michael does."

"Would you ever own a donkey?"

"What? No, of course not."

The guy glanced up and grinned. "That isn't a real question. I just like to lighten the mood. This doesn't have to be a scary process."

You clearly had to be an insider to get immigration humor.

We were in there for another twenty minutes answering a barrage of random but mostly predictable questions and then we were finally sprung when our interviewer got a phone call.

Downstairs we stepped outside to a sunny and hot day in June. I put my hand on the small of Felicia's back.

I knew exactly what she would say first. I could guarantee it.

"He didn't even look at my scrapbook," she complained.

Yep. That's what I thought she would say.

I put on sunglasses and peeled off my suit jacket. I had to go back to work. I still had a full afternoon of patient appointments. "I can't stop picturing you as a spy. Can we role-play tonight?"

She laughed. "Sure. The world's most elusive and pregnant spy for the Crown. Don't be an idiot."

I leaned in close and gave her a kiss. "I'll be your American contact and your code name for me can be Daddy."

Her mouth rounded into an O. "I see. I think arrangements can be made, then."

Then her phone rang in her hand. Distracted, she glanced at it. "It's the interviewer."

She answered and there was a lot of "uh-huhs" and then she grinned and ended the call. "I'm in," she said. "Visa approved."

"Are you serious? Just like that?"

"It had to be the scrapbook. Our engagement photos were to die for."

"Of course that was it. I never doubted it." I gave her another kiss. "I never doubted *us*."

Thank you for reading Forty Day Fiancé!
Want more rom com?
One-click Kindle Unlimited standalone read with a Happily Ever
After!

Weekend Wife
Billionaire businessman in need of a fake fiancée...

It should be the easiest job ever for an out-of-work actress, right?

All I have to do is pose as Grant Caldwell (the Third)'s fiancée for a fancy-pants weekend in the Hamptons. Easy. Wear designer clothing and sip champagne? Don't mind if I do. Flirting with Grant? It's so delicious I should be paying *him*.

Nothing can go wrong as long as I can just keep my hands off of him.

But that's the hard part. And I do mean *hard*.

Because Grant is sexy.
And bossy.
And surprisingly sweet, a real rarity in his pretentious family.

Oops. I'm not as good at faking it as I thought. Or maybe they call this method acting. Because it's getting harder to figure out where my character ends and I begin...

It just might be the role of a lifetime.

ABOUT THE AUTHOR

USA Today and New York Times Bestselling author Erin McCarthy sold her first book in 2002 and has since written almost eighty novels and novellas in the romance and mystery genres. Erin has a special weakness for tattoos, high-heeled boots, and martinis. She lives with her renovation-addicted husband and their blended family of kids and rescue dogs.

.

Made in the USA
Middletown, DE
02 June 2020

96510044R00130